# The Ties That Bind

by
Vanessa Duriès

The Ties That Bind
Copyright ©2005 by Magic Carpet Books, Inc.
All Rights Reserved

No part of this book may be reproduced,
stored in a retrieval system, or transmitted in any form,
by any means, including mechanical, electronic,
photocopying, recording or otherwise, without
prior written permission from the publisher and author.

First Magic Carpet Books, Inc. edition October 2005

Published in 2005

Manufactured in the United States of America
Published by Magic Carpet Books, Inc.

Magic Carpet Books, Inc.
PO Box 473
New Milford, CT 06776

Library of Congress Cataloging in Publication Date

The Ties That Bind by Vanessa Duriés
$14.95

ISBN# 0-9766510-1-7
Book Design: P. Ruggieri

# Table of Contents

Introduction by Maria Isabel Pita....5

Prologue....11

I The Revelation....17

II The Rules of the Game....25

III The First Evening....31

IV The Reprimand....39

V The Test....49

VI The Ink of Fantasies....63

VII The Pride of the Slave....75

VIII The Captivating Cellar....79

IX Failures....93

X Slaughtering....99

XI The Chastity Belt....109

XII Prostitution....117

XIII Spleen....127

XIV The Golden Rings...133

XV The Black Notebook....141

Afterward: *Photographs of Vanessa*....147
by Maxim Jakubowski

# Introduction

by
Maria Isabel Pita

There's something perversely enchanted about *The Ties That Bind* in which Vanessa Duriès lives forever suspended in ideal submission to her master's desires; blessed at birth with an intelligent mind, a beautiful body and a passionate soul able to fulfill his every sadistic wish. The perfect slave is indeed like a fairytale princess in the utterly trusting, inescapable way she submits to the physically violent and emotionally sinister trials set before her, all for the sake of true love – for her master, who is both the all-knowing author and the hero of her darkest fantasies. Vanessa died tragically young in a car crash, shortly after she wrote this book which gives rise to a thorny forest of questions those of us who dare embrace the S&M lifestyle must all get through somehow. For most of us, if we're fortunate, the journey takes years, and demands the exercise of all the mysterious inner powers we possess.

The first painful question I asked myself after reading Vanessa's shockingly intense memoir was, inevitably: what would have become of her, and of her relationship with her master, if she had lived and grown older? She died a very young woman who passionately believed in the profound virtues of her unorthodox lifestyle. Her words have the indelible ring of truth, so in a sense it doesn't matter that her experiences were cut short because what is true is eternal and cannot be violated by time. And yet, what if…?

What if Vanessa had lived a long life? "Sadomasochism is an art, a philosophy, a cultural space" she says, meaning it is open to interpretation, development, growth, all of life's qualities in which change is inevitable and healthy. What if Vanessa had lived and remained with her master? How long could they have continued engaging in the activities she so frankly and proudly describes? What the body feels to be true when it is young differs from the perceptions of older flesh; even if her philosophy of Sadomasochism had not changed, how long could her body have kept the faith? Vanessa likens herself to an athlete when she is enduring the agonizing abuse her master and his friends subject her to. She is proud of her ability to withstand the pain with dignity, and she even manages sometimes to perform a perverse alchemy in the mysterious crucible of her sex and transform the torture into ecstasy. The problem is that an athlete's career, no matter how illustrious, comes to an end eventually. For how many years could Vanessa's beautiful body, trained and pushed to extremes, have preserved the proud detachment of an athlete during the many tortures inflicted upon it?

Vanessa was with her master such a short time, but what if they had stayed together for years – as all men and women profoundly in love hope to do no matter their lifestyle – could she have remained content with "the mental structure of a slave" once her flesh seriously began to protest? And there was more than physical pain for her to contend with; there was the misery of jealousy, which she was always suffering as a result of her master's love of beauty. The bond she shared with him was uniquely special, and precisely because of this his "meaningless" infidelities caused her a much deeper discomfort than anything else. Vanessa speaks about the "pride of the slave", and there is no doubt she loved the fact that as a young and beautiful submissive she was always the center of attention. "I became again what I wanted to be, a simple object at the service of the master I loved, the object that every man could lust after, surrendered to the pleasure of my Master who could dispose of me and give my body to whoever he wanted." It seems telling that she was working on a manuscript entitled The Rivals when she was killed, a book about the rivalry between two submissive women. Was she already struggling to remain the center of her master's attention? We will never know, yet it's impossi-

## The Ties That Bind

ble not to notice that the older women Vanessa intimately encounters are all dominant personalities. How long would she have been content to remain "a simple object" if she had lived and matured? Would the dynamic of Pierre and Vanessa's love for each other have weathered the changes in a relationship gradually but inevitably wrought by time and the mellowing refinements of age?

We will never know the answers, yet it is the questions that are vitally important. To all those living in a master and slave relationship, and to everyone interested in truly exploring the lifestyle, *The Ties That Bind* offers an arousing embodiment, and a breathtaking affirmation, of S&M's profound ideals, even while raising challenging questions about how the lifestyle can be sustained throughout a long and healthy life in a loving relationship.

# The Ties That Bind

## Prologue

At the age of nine I was a fairly lively little girl, brown-haired, with a face like a shrew. I did not regard myself as particularly pretty, but I overheard some compliments about myself at family reunions. Sometimes I lent an attentive ear to the conversations of adults. I have never been more disobedient than my sisters, or my brother, and I have no memory of having been a particularly difficult child. However, and I have never understood why, my father often treated me either as a shameless hussy or a little slut. I wasn't particularly brazen, but he hounded me as if I had committed the worst offences. I hadn't the least notion of sin, and for a long time I strained my imagination to picture what distinguished an ordinary brat, like my classmates or my sisters, from the little slut that I was said to be.

## The Ties That Bind

The first memory of punishments that my father inflicted on me goes back to exactly that time. He had bound me, hand and foot, in the corridor of the magnificent house that we lived in, following some misdemeanor. I was treated that evening to a severe thrashing, which marked my body and memory to such a degree that today I still think of those first blows, that first terror, and my first real suffering as an innocent victim.

My father had the habit of beating me for the tiniest thing, or if I snubbed him in the slightest way. Then he would get hold of one of his alarming, and always impeccably polished and shiny black shoes, or the chestnut brown crocodile belt that my sisters and I had given him for a Father's Day or Christmas present, and would deal me several violent and well-aimed blows that reached the most sensitive parts of my body.

When he was in a very cruel mood, he would lock me inside a cupboard, tied up in the dark; its cramped nature terrifying me. His enormous and powerful male hands would come down on my emaciated face, turning it crimson immediately, like a distress signal at a shipwreck. These unfair punishments humiliated me deeply at the start. But, inexplicably, the more they were repeated, the more I had a strange feeling which progressed from troubling to disgusting me, and ended up completely destabilizing my relationship with my father, though I could never manage to hate him. Looking back today, I think I felt the pride then that she who is the object of the cruelty of a loved one experiences. Each blow received can thus be interpreted as a mark of interest, even of love. Because, if not, why would the father or the master inflict punishment? Why would either whip his child, his slave?

Clearly, I was still ignorant of all the conflicting pleasures that the one who strikes can give to the one who receives the blows. I was only a little scared girl. But even then I refused, with all my will, the predisposition of my feminine state, which made me the victim of a man.

I have only resigned myself to the destiny that I have freely chosen. Not having the nature of an Amazon, not knowing how to oppose violence with cruelty, I learnt to dominate those who used me by making the offering of my submission both mystical and ambiguous.

This is how slaves live. They are the only ones to hold the keys to the dark and dank cellars where the fantasies of the masters hoist them to the ranks of deities.

# I – The Revelation

I am not sentimental, yet I love my Master and do not hide the fact. He is everything that is intelligent, charming and strict. Of course, like every self-respecting master, he sometimes appears very demanding, which pains and irritates me when he pushes me to the limits of my moral and physical resistance.

My Master is impassioned, and he lives only for his passion: sadomasochism. This philosophy, for it is one, represents in his eyes an ideal way of life, but I am resolutely opposed to that view. One cannot, one must not be a sadomasochist the whole time. The grandeurs and constraints of everyday life do not live happily with fantasies. One must know how to protect one from the other by separating them openly. When the master and the slave live together, they must have

## The Ties That Bind

the wisdom to alternate the sufferings and the languors, the delights and the torments. In matters of sadomasochism, standardization is intolerable. A breathing space is of prime importance.

My Master is a man of experience, unlike me, a young slave of twenty, initiated only a few months ago. The experience, which my Master shows, chills me sometimes, to tell the truth, as if unconsciously I am annoyed that he has evolved without me for more than thirteen years in the practice of that cerebral art.

I am a masochist. He is a pure and hard sadist, and his knowledge in that field which today one calls, much too commonly, 'SM', fascinates me to the highest degree.

He can obtain all of me, force me, put into concrete form all that he desires or dares not even confess. I am guided by the trust that I show him. Blind trust where I am made truly blind with a band or a leather mask covering my eyes, when I must submit to various trials, in places and with third parties known to him alone.

The trust which unites the master and his slave is fundamental, it conditions and authorizes all excesses; that is to say, all happiness.

I love him and I know that he loves me to the point of being certain that that love will never lead us astray onto dangerous paths where one cannot turn back. It is that experience that I wanted to recount in this book with, of course, the authorization and encouragement of my Master. He sees in this confession a new trial that I must overcome in order to merit the title and rank that I occupy beside him.

The revelation occurred the first time I ventured into the apartment of the one who was going to become my Master and my love. I felt no fear, even though I am very shy, on discovering the straps hanging from the beams, the photos conspicuous on the sycamore drawers, placed as defiant provocation to the little naive and innocent virgin that I still was.

Pierre was attentive, with a courtesy that I had not known previously with boys of my own age who hung around me. Pierre was a reassuring man, a man whose success and social standing was the best token of security that I could imagine at that time.

I was very impressed at the sight of all those initiatory objects whose use I was ignorant of, for the most part, but from which I could not turn away. My imagination carried me into a world that I feared without being able to grasp its subtleties. These noble accessories of leather, steel or latex spoke to me: they evoked my childhood surprisingly by arousing the same anguish, the same delicious fear that I experienced when returning to the house where a punishment perhaps awaited me. A mixture of curiosity and distress surged within me. The unexpected is a weapon of seduction. It was not without reason that Pierre led me to discover his ritual objects. He knew that I avoided the banal more than anything. Anything that is out of the ordinary catches my eye, grabs my attention and draws me irresistibly towards it.

The accessories of domination can appear, when one ignores their dangers and pleasantries, as evidence of a questionable taste. How can

## The Ties That Bind

a man as distinguished in appearance, as conventional in conduct, dare to decorate his environment with objects of torture in this manner? The exhibition of almost surgical material—forceps, speculums, rings and so on—should have served to terrify and urge me to flee this sex maniac. But, on the contrary, this display reassured me through its frankness, awakening a deep unease within me.

Pierre behaved just as he is in reality: direct, sincere, without deviating and, above all, without lies. Instinctively I trusted him. I might have appeared to have surrendered to curiosity. Something in me drove me to know this man better and to commend my soul to him. In actual fact, I had the feeling of walking alone in the night for far too long. I felt a genuine relief in being sure that I had finally met my guide.

For a moment, I caught sight of myself in a mirror which hung on a wall in the room. Before me stood a young woman of twenty with dark and curly hair, an intense hard look, and full lips like those of a child. I looked at my body as the one of a rival: back straightened, but a little too large; delicate bust weighed down by round and heavy breasts whose nipples pointed permanently toward the heavens, as if to implore it. This student, 'good class, good family', who frequented the university, was not supposed to hang around in this kind of place, or in the company of this kind of character.

Despite the leather, steel and latex, I stayed with him that evening. I no longer leave the house and I have become the attentive partner of my Master. Because, in truth, if I have the taste for adventure, if I seek the unexpected, I like above all to feel frightened. That undoubtedly explains my behavior. The game of unusual situations excites and seduces me. The danger, or what I imagine, intoxicates me, plunges me into a semi-conscious state where my whole being allows itself to split in two, forgetting all the constraints imposed by an extremely strict upbringing. It is me without being me. I sincerely think that kind of schizophrenia permits me to liberate certain repressed impulses. The double game makes me not guilty.

I have a reserved nature. My friends know my shyness and lack of self-confidence despite my attraction to certain adventures. Until my meeting with Pierre, it was difficult to imagine me in situations that I judged scandalous. I would never have dared, at that time, to play the role of a prostitute. I would have refused, pleading that this role did not suit me because it was not part of my fantasies. My experiences with Pierre have taught me this: if I was incapable of becoming a good and authentic whore, I was delighted to play that role for the pleasure of my lover. His pride at my submission gave me an exaltation close to orgasm. Was that then only to feel the satisfaction of the loved man? Or, already, was it the reality of surrendering myself without conditions to a social taboo, and then transgressing it, with the alibi of pleasing my lover and acting on his orders, that made me aware of such incredible sensations? Was it the humiliation of being called a little whore which gave me that pleasure, or the incredible escape into a world in which I would never have dared to penetrate all alone, without Him?

## The Ties That Bind

I have learnt to cry out loud and strong that I am a whore, a bitch, when a stranger takes me beneath the eyes of my Master. I proclaim then that I am a slut and I know how to become one when I really desire it. To keep apace of my female instinct makes me come constantly, above all when I know my Master is attentive to the slightest contact, to the slightest humiliation on the part of men to whom he delivers me.

One of the greatest joys of life is to be able to liquidate the taboos which live in us. I know nothing more enriching about self-knowledge than to attain it.

# II – The Rules of the Game

The game of relationships between the master and his slave is subtle and delicate. Slaves must know how to indicate the limits to the masters so as not to exceed them. Absolute authority is a clever game of balance, the slightest false step breaks the harmony and shatters the respect that one feels for the other. All human beings have their limits, slaves have their own. No master can go beyond the limits, morally or physically, accepted by their slave. Any deviation from this rule can be fatal.

In this, the role of the master is extremely difficult to adhere to, because he must adapt to the personality and capacity for obedience and resistance of each slave. One or the other must never disappoint. The slave must grant to the master the privileges of his function: to

## The Ties That Bind

give him the intoxicating happiness to dominate a receptive and obedient being who knows to prove herself once in a while of her independence, who can disobey with discernment, because the punishment which ensues will be the source of pleasure for both one and the other. To know how to disobey is an art which implicates a perfect knowledge of the desires of the master, without mentioning love, since it is the word that no one pronounces in the course of these contests.

The game hinges on this exceptional relationship of force. To submit, disobey, endure, these delicate choices that I do not want to escape. The tension must never cease to increase. The role of slave is always to give herself completely to whoever is the person responsible for her training and whatever its practices. Resistance to humiliations, to constraints, to suffering increases the intensity and the cerebral aspect of the combat. It is then that my body can bloom, can give in its entirety. That's the ecstasy, the exacerbated enjoyment through the often unexpected rites, the self-denial that one keeps constantly present, for submission to the other, for suffering also. It is precisely that unknown part which fascinates me, which fascinates the slave, because in sadomasochist relationships, the ingenuity of the master must be renewed constantly and put to the test. It is very exciting to be always unaware of what can occur in the course of a session, never to foresee the surprises that the master reserves for you. It can happen that a slave loaned by the one to whom she belongs proves more performable with another master than with her own. Even skin contact with one person can electrify you then whereas another may leave you indifferent. Privileged masters communicate with their slave, while others remain obstinately foreign, non-existent, artificial.

My great happiness is to have found a Master suitable for me, who waits for what I can give him precisely, who gives me everything that I am entitled to wait for.

If the role of master demands a creativity out of the ordinary to vary the demands, the slave must show a great physical resistance. The intense pressure that my Master exerts on me leads me sometimes to requestion my personality and interrogate myself about myself. Will I be equal to his demands? Shall I reach the level of perfection which can sublimate our perilous relationship?

It is essential for me to be able to give myself without reservation, without expecting anything in return except to merit the rank and title of slave chosen above all; to regret nothing, to provoke no reproach, to offer the best image of myself, or more simply, to give myself over. The slave is by definition very sensitive to the manner in which she is treated, even if humiliation is indistinguishable from the pleasure that she gains. I am extremely sensitive to the opinion that my Master can have of me. Fear of disappointing him through refusal pushes me sometimes to accept certain trials which repulse me, but attests to my belonging to him. To give happiness (to accept all from him, blindly) to the man that I love is a major preoccupation for me, much more exalting than the realisation of my own masochistic fantasies. My Master knows this and sometimes has the tendency to abuse the situation of dependence engendered through love that I bear him by forcing me to accept each of the humiliations, each of the trials he imposes on me.

If he pushes me sometimes to the paroxysm of exhaustion and physical suffering during very trying sessions, bringing me to the limit of a psychological breakdown, it is enough for me to look at him and become aware of his pleasure. That is sufficient to increase my strength.

It is fairly obvious that the uninitiated are ignorant of this marginal and captivating world. The master is never the person that one imagines. The master is in a state of total dependence in relation to his slave. The master exists and only finds his place or his justification in relation to the slave. He is in reality the slave of the slave, of her acceptance to submit to the cruelties which excite him. When one has understood this paradoxical reality, there is no more shame to being a slave. On the contrary, through the subtle game of relationships of strength, the slave can be the one who exerts the true power in the sadomasochist relationship.

# III – The First Evening

All Pierre had said was that we would go to Bordeaux, to the house of a couple older than us. That first experience of initiation into sadomasochism was to unfold inside a vaulted cellar specially prepared for the purpose.

Until then, I sensed my taste for masochism without knowing where it would lead me with Pierre. Before I met him, my relationships had been very conventional. I was ignorant of everything in that field, and my apprehension was on a par with my curiosity.

After a journey which seemed interminable, we arrived at the town. Crossroads and lights succeeded one another until the car became jammed in a street so narrow it made me think of a thieves' alley where I would never have dared to venture alone. I was so afraid

## The Ties That Bind

I began to tremble. My heart beat hard and my breathing became breathless. Pierre stopped the car before a severe-looking door where a man with an imposing stature awaited us. It was time to repress my anxiety and I found myself blindfolded before the colossus. My Master tied my hands behind my back. A strong and brutal grip encircled my frail arms and led me into a room that I imagined was tiny and plunged in total darkness, a kind of antechamber where I waited a long time, perhaps half an hour or more, in a state of anguish and extreme excitement. Suddenly a presence appeared and snatched me from my torpor. I was pushed onto a small winding staircase. The smell of wet earth filled my nostrils. At the bottom was a cellar with its characteristic smell of mould. The true cellar for the slave to love.

A voice ordered me to introduce myself, which I did instantly. For me to do this, my hands were unfastened. Then I parted my thighs and straightened my back, as my Master had ordered me, in order to offer with the greatest indecency the spectacle of my intimacy, as none had yet discovered it. So that all the spectators could appreciate my obedience, I turned around slowly. I was still blindfolded and fear gripped me all of a sudden. Voices filled the space, though I was incapable of saying how many people were there. Five or six, perhaps more.

A finger prodded me from behind and penetrated me violently. Surprised by the pain, I reacted with insolence by attempting to escape the finger that continued to insinuate itself in me. The one who violated me thus, without preparation, threatened me harshly. I disobeyed again my disengaging myself with reckless motions that finally freed me.

A long silence followed, disturbed only by the whisperings which I tried in vain to discern. Without being able to defend myself, I felt myself lifted from the floor, and my wrists and ankles bound forcefully to a cross. In that position, which favored the examination of my body, the finger forced itself afresh into my anus, drawing from me a genuine cry of horror and pain of which I am today still ashamed. I straightened myself with all my strength. The finger withdrew as brutally as it had entered and ventured along my lips, which were parted, so that my mouth was impregnated with the bitter taste of my own cavity. I could not surpress a feeling of disgust, principally caused by the humiliation I felt. My repugnance was such that I felt myself ready to quit and flee. Abandoned in that ignominious posture, I was conscious of my lack of discipline. Five minutes had barely elapsed since my arrival. I had no right to let myself go through fear, even if all this ritual seemed insupportable to the poor inexperienced slave that I was then. The perspective of knowing my Master was appalled and displeased with me convinced me to submit myself and I calmed down as best I could by imposing on myself an absolute stillness.

After quite some time, which sharpened again my nerves—though, this time, I let nothing show, forbidding myself the least movement—they withdrew the blindfold.

I saw a young submissive girl, barely older than me. Someone called her "Number Seven." I never found out why. She appeared on the verge of exhaustion and, examining her more carefully, I noted that she had a perfect body and the tender face of a well-behaved little girl.

A man, whose face I was unable to see, spoke to her and referred to her as a "bag of fuck." I discovered later that she was there to serve as the receptacle for the semen of the masters, that she received it through every orifice provided by nature, without ever protesting or even betraying any feeling whatever. She was a woman degraded to the rank of object, dumb and servile.

However, I noticed one thing that the other participants regarded as negligible: Number Seven was on the verge of tears and her pretty lips were trembling with emotion.

Then one of the men murmured in her ear, his hand stroking the pretty neck that curved beneath his caress, telling her that she must make use of the beautiful young virgin that I was still, in whatever way she wished.

At that time I had no homosexual experience, and I felt a certain repulsion that the idea of having physical relations with a woman, even one as young and pretty as this. Inexplicably, she began to cry, as if the hand of the master had triggered her sobs, which now shook that frail female body, a body that was submissive to the whims of men. She was pitiful, and the suffering I read at that moment in her look appeased my anxiety. I began to cry also and we poured out bitter tears, face to face, providing a spectacle as peculiar as it was intolerable for the demanding masters.

Number Seven appeared to calm herself and rapidly resumed a

more dignified attitude, hiding her emotions until the end of the evening. She departed with a man, who took her by the arm, and I found myself alone, guilty, with the terrible feeling of having committed an unpardonable offence which would deprive me, perhaps forever, of the respect and love of my Master.

My penitence in the damp cellar was prolonged beyond the three hours, increasing my disarray and fear. Three trying and terrifying hours, during which I envisaged my dishonour, and my death, perhaps. I was delirious. And then a man approached me and spoke softly. His whisperings calmed me. Master Georges showed me patience, curious to know about my experiences and motivations. When he knew that I was right then in the process of my initiation, he had the kindness to express his understanding of my attitude and promised I would not incur any punishment.

He permitted me to rest and made me stretch out on a kind of low couch where I regained confidence in myself. After a while, when he came in search of me, my doubts and fears were appeased.

This start to the initiation was not without repercussions on the mood of Pierre, concerned for the most scrupulous perfection in the submission and obedience that his slaves had to show on every occasion. I know that he was reputed for his implacable severity and, in this status, sought by the real and truly experienced masters who were always surrounded by hardened associates.

# IV – The Reprimand

had not been perfect, far from it. I let myself sink into a moment of weakness, and he probably did not pardon me. I now had to face a new initiation, trials far more testing still: reproaches and humiliations that he was going to create to punish me. Pierre called me a little incompetent slut, pretentious and without honor. I had failed in my word. He was insulting me and that made me feel sick. His anger was unjust, quite as much as my avoidance was unworthy of the love that I felt for him.

My Master had to remember that the first time is always difficult to endure, that the apprenticeship of sadomasochist relationships puts one's own integrity into question.

I believe that the intervention of Master Georges saved us from

## The Ties That Bind

disaster. What would I have done if he had not come near me, placed his arm around my waist to reassure me? Perhaps I would have left, shame-faced and mortified. Perhaps my experience would have been limited to that occasion alone.

Having dragged me to the depths of the cellar, where the semi-darkness was densest, he flung my body against the wet wall. I felt the saltpeter crumble beneath my clinging fingers. To redeem myself I almost wanted to be bound, there, in that position, belly naked against that sticky wall, back, hips, offered to men who would have me at their disposal, without conditions. To feel my hands grip the stone, no longer to be able to move and to endure all, to prove that I was able to become one day a perfect slave, envied by all the masters, the object of pride of the only one I venerated.

Master Georges began to caress me. He knew by doing this he gave me a chance to make my offence forgotten. He took hold of a strap and worked on my body, heating it up slowly, alternating the caresses of the thin strip with cruel and violent blows. The harder he struck me, the more I offered myself. I felt a sharp twinge at the moment my breasts were brutally gripped by pincers, and then I felt the nipples crushed by the metal vice which tugged them towards the ground, hanging. Each movement I made increased the swaying of the pincers, provoking a frightful wrenching sensation.

I remember the moment precisely when I was placed on all fours in the middle of the cellar. The master of whom I was the slave for the evening fixed other pincers to the lips of my sex, right below the clitoris.

My whole body swayed in an obscene fashion, racked between two pains, divided between the desire to make my suffering cease and the other to increase the intensity through swaying, in order to satisfy my Master and merit his pardon. I observed with pride the swaying of the weights suspended by the pincers attached to my breasts, from right to left, from left to right. The pain became intolerable, but I became the spectator of that pain. I suffered, but I dominated that suffering. The pleasure which rose insidiously within me exceeded it, stigmatized it.

Thus I experienced the first cerebral orgasm of a woman submissive to a man who obliges her to suffer. Something indefinable seemed to have taken control of my brain and commanded my body to come from that flashing suffering, magnified by my servile obedience. This was an amazing revelation for me which succeeded in freeing me from that imposed and deliberate pain inflicted by the master to whom I was lent as an object without importance, without worth, which I had become by refusing my first trial.

To mark his satisfaction, Master Georges pointed to the Saint Andrew's Cross, where I was tied in the position of perfect quartering. Pierre approached me then, as if I had become once again deserving of his interest, and I thought I read in his look the love he gives me sometimes, a little awkwardly, but which reassures me so much and which is my reason for being. They each seized long whips and began to flagellate me with a vigor and rhythm which opened my eyes wide. In order to stifle my howls, I bit my lips hard, until the taste of my own blood had filled my mouth.

## The Ties That Bind

I surrendered myself to the chastisement with a joy that was almost mystical, with the faith of a consecrated being. In my considerably overheated mind, troubled by that succession of fears, sufferings, and intermingled pleasures, I could no longer make out the difference between one and the other. Flashing images of sacrifices surged in me. I wanted to be the lamb offered on the altar. I surprised myself by whispering "thank you" at each fresh blow, and what did it matter if my flesh tore, if my blood flowed, if my legs suddenly gave way, brutally forcing all the weight of my tortured body onto my shoulders and painfully fragile wrists?

I had regained the esteem of my Master. I had become a slave worthy of this name and worthy of her master. And there is no greater happiness than to know one is appreciated. It is a little like love, with a dizzy thrill in addition.

In the deserted cellar, where the dampness reminded me of a tomb, a man approached me. He looked at me silently, and I noticed that he held two long and thin needles. I don't remember his face. It's rare enough for me to remember the faces of men whose slave I have been. I retain only fleeting impressions of those to whom Pierre has offered me. I would probably be incapable of recognizing any of those who have been my master for one night in the street, as if, immediately after the rite, my mind wishes to evacuate all strangers in order to keep only the image of a couple reunited in a common passion, an extreme complicity, without equal between my Master and I.

The sight of the needles reawakened my fears, but I encouraged myself by saying that my new stature as slave authorized the most severe trials. I decided I no longer had the right to be afraid, and from that moment on, a form of serenity took hold of me and permitted me to exteriorize a form of indifference which flattered both my Master and the man who came to torment me.

The man with the needles took hold of a breast, which he began to knead, to caress, then to pinch in order to make the granulose nipple swell. When the nipple was truly excited, he stuck in his first needle, then, almost immediately, he stuck in the second in the nipple of the breast which had not been caressed and which reacted in a totally different manner. Thus I had proof that excitation attenuates the suffering and transforms it into a diffuse sensation. Arriving at that verification, I concluded that, like a breast properly caressed, a loved and glorified slave can accept and endure all, nourished by the sole passion for her master. Other needles were inserted all around my areola. Some drops of blood tarnished the metal that the lights made gleam. In order to increase, doubtlessly, the extent of my suffering, the torturer pierced the skin around my sex. I felt a kind of repulsion. The sight of those pieces of metal forcing resistance from my epidermis in order to plunge through my flesh, to dig into the tissue of muscles, to come out again further with a drop of blood, made my heart swell. But I forced myself to chase away those images worthy of a horror film to think only of Pierre, who assisted in my torture as a connoisseur. With each needle piercing my skin, I cried out within: "Master, I love you with all my heart, and my love permits me to endure these awful sufferings. Thank you, Master, for permitting me to love you in this way. Your love is my strength and permits me to conquer what I believed impossible until this evening."

Without being aware, too preoccupied to probe my limits for fear of not being able to exceed myself, I arrived at the paroxysm of excitement. My sex seemed to contain and concentrate all the enjoyment that I could still not reach with orgasms. Pleasure boiled beneath my skin as if my whole body was liquefied and was going to spill out. My guts were on fire, I consumed myself. Without doubt it was not only the sensation of pleasure, but reality itself.

Master Patrick, leaning over me, held a candle in his hand. Slowly, the small gilt candlestick was inclined and the burning wax pearled on my skin in big whitish lumps. The idea of being burnt alive increased my excitement. My martyrdom became delicious. I lost all notion of time and pain. I awaited what followed in a state close to unconsciousness.

The lashes of the whips of the three men cut me suddenly with a terrifying violence. I guessed that these abominably cruel lashes were destined to burst the small crusts of wax that studded my belly and breasts. I was unable to hold back further. My back straightened, propelling my thighs and belly forward, like the dying throes of an electrocuted person, releasing an orgasm so violent that I believed I would break that cross that held me prisoner. Ashamed and proud, I had come beneath the treatments inflicted by the simple will of my Master.

I don't know what followed. I seem to remember a crowd around me, and the pleasure that those witnesses discharged on my body. I remember a look, a rose offered by a young submissive that my initiation seemed to have unsettled. He gave me that flower—which I keep in memory of that first night—and whispered these words:

"Because roses have not been created only for suffering, I offer this to you."

Much later I persuaded myself of the extreme cruelty of roses.

# V – The Test

Pierre is an organizer beyond compare. Since sharing his life, we schedule usually quite eventful weekends throughout the year. When we return, on Sunday evenings, I often find myself in a state close to exhaustion. Pierre is no less tired than me. The role of master is exhausting, because, while the slave only submits, the master must decide, organize, prepare and take action, all the while watching over the physical and psychic state of the slave that he has decided to honor through tests and humiliations.

And that was how we spent a weekend in a town in the north, at the house of a couple of very experienced dominants who are among those closest to Pierre. They are both fifty, and we like them for their refinement, their good manners and their experience in a form

# The Ties That Bind

of very elaborate sadomasochism.

Pierre claims that their sensitivity is such that they adapt easily to the slave who is delivered to them, which is unfortunately not always the case with others. Too often, the bad master uses the loaned slave to gorge his vulgar sexual desires. Refinement in the matter is to utilize the psychology of the object-being in order to discover true fantasies. Mine are to celebrate the value of my Master, who has revealed to me my true nature, my obvious predestination to submission. Others have the transgression of taboos for fantasies that they have never had the courage to confront without the excuse of slavery. One woman desiring coprophagy could not fulfill that practice except in the secret world of leather, steel and latex. This creature of dreams, who I had seem delivered to a group of Africans, in a parking lot near Lyons, is in everyday life an elegant computer expert who only becomes a receptacle for a few hours a week, through the goodwill of the master who authorizes her to act out her most secret aspirations. Because, if there is one thing which I can bear witness to, despite my insignificant experience, it is this: one never imposes on a slave what she does not want to do. In the world of sadomasochism, the slave chooses with the agreement of her master the tests and rites which she desires to submit to for their common happiness. The other cases, which they speak about sometimes in the gutter press, have nothing to do with the authentic 'SM', but rise purely and simply from blood sports.

The local amenities provided by our northern friends were very disagreeable and very sophisticated. The organization of the house, from cellar to attic, had been conceived for the activities which interest us.

Pierre had prepared me to handle the important events that would take place in the course of the weekend. I was terribly anxious to find myself faced by a couple of experienced dominants, who had practiced the rites of sadomasochism for more years than I myself had lived. Once again, my main fear was that I would not have the strength and willpower to prove myself equal to the tests by which they were going to judge me and, through me, my Master. In any case, I had to give the best of myself, and to consider, in the worst situations that I would be faced with, the invaluable chance which was offered me to follow an instruction the same as those in the houses of masters famous throughout Europe, without even having been presented to them before, and without them ever before having tested my true aptitudes.

By entering into that world, for me magical, I repeated to myself that I had no right to deceive anybody, neither Pierre nor his friends, who gave me the honor of being received into the ranks of the 'privileged'. Maïté and Julien came to fetch us from the airport. I didn't dare to look at them directly. I lowered my eyes, a sign of submission, as Pierre had instructed me. We climbed into their car and, throughout the whole journey, I did not utter a single word, contenting myself by caressing Pierre with tenderness and respect. He was my only point of reference, my only point of attachment. I had the impression that I would be able to face anything with him, to show

## The Ties That Bind

myself in the strongest light and the mere contact of his hand in mine made me feel happy and reassured me. How sweet it was for me to escape into slavery, for a few hours that I guessed would be exhausting, in the arms of my beloved Master!

After a brief stop at the hotel, where we left our luggage, we arrived finally at the house, the 'SM manor' as I liked to call it.

I was very excited, my heart beat strongly as I couldn't wait to enter the house. I was imagining the architecture and interior decoration from Pierre's previous descriptions. I was curious to know if my imagination conformed with reality.

When the front door closed behind me, my disappointment was acute. I stared around wide-eyed and surveyed the rooms that they led me through. There was not the slightest trace of appliances, accessories, or even the shadow of a SM environment.

I was deceived and no longer knew what to believe. Was it possible that Pierre had completely invented the magic place that he had described so well and at such length?

That first evening lasted about three hours. It was my official debut under the name of 'Laïka,' which was going to become my pseudonym for all our sadomasochist activities. According to the rite dear to the initiated, it is the master who presents his slave, so that his hosts can take account of her real limits and so utilize her to her best advantage afterwards.

According to Pierre's instructions, I raised my dress and spread my legs, straightening my back as I liked to do. That increased the curve of my hips and emphasized the contours of my buttocks, shaped like apples.

Presenting oneself in this way obliges the slave to undress and offer her body to show its faults; to get to know itself better, to accept itself more. Through this nakedness, the body is surrendered, undressed, dissected, as if ridiculed, humiliated, and without concession. The slave exhibited in this way learns the power of her body and she draws her strength from the fascination that the master feels for her.

My skin submitted immediately to the contact, with cold hands placed in the hollow of my back, then between my buttocks. These unknown hands, feared and yet awaited, examined me, caressed me pleasantly, as if they wanted at the same time to know everything about my shape and my thoughts. I opened my thighs further so that the attentive hands could discover everything that they inspected. When the master who tested me was perfectly convinced of my absolute obedience, the masters joined together and undertook other games.

A black riding-crop cut me abruptly and with such violence that I let out a genuine howl. It's known that the alternation of sweetness and violence tends to break in the reticent slave. But me, a poor beginner eager to do well for the happiness of my Master, I knew nothing of all that and believed I was being punished for an offence committed unbeknown to me. Had I displeased by my position? My look, despite myself, would it be regarded as insolent? My mouth, without wishing it, had it suggested I could challenge the tests? Had I the right to beg for pity? Couldn't I present my excuses to my Master and his hosts? The rigidity of the riding-crop inflamed my hips and my back. The blows lacerated my flesh, shooting burning sensations through me. I had fallen out of the habit of being whipped as I had been deprived of it for at least a good month. Sometimes Pierre promised to whip me, as if it were a reward. So I began to await the crop like a testimony of satisfaction: what does it matter then that it concerns the satisfaction of the master or the slave…

Imperceptibly, the pain appeared to lessen and give way to a sensation of diffuse pleasure that is difficult for me to explain. One can compare it to the feeling one experiences when one withdraws a splinter from a finger, and that through the intolerable pain one glimpses the alleviation. The blows becoming lighter, more controlled. I realized suddenly that I was about to come. When the staff of the crop reached between my thighs, onto the bulge of the pubis, I felt the big and delicious shame of allowing myself to groan, bending my legs slightly to tighten my thighs. I experienced an orgasm that delighted my Master and his hosts. What had really happened?

My body, my skin, did they really delight in suffering? Or else did my subconscious transform that suffering into orgasm? In fact, I was no more than a body and an abandoned will in my submission to the loved one.

Once the fulgurating orgasm dissipated, I felt the pain return to rack me and, with a rare unconsciousness, I ventured to implore their pity. The masters looked at each other, deceived and disconcerted. After a brief discussion with contemptuous whisperings, the masters decided to make me pay dearly for that unjustifiable weakness. I had broken the spell, I had interrupted the ecstasy of eminent flagellants. I was led to the first floor, where everyone decided to take me without consideration.

Mistress Maïté led me. I was placed to the wall that contained a hole in its middle so that my head passed through to one side and left my hips on the other. I was going to be taken by the rear and compelled by the mouth simultaneously. Maïté settled me. I was in position, legs obediently spread, rump exaggeratedly offered, mouth open and waiting, ready to be invested according to the goodwill of my masters. Seeing me thus submissive, their anger abated. Pierre approached and spoke tenderly:

"I'm proud of you. You're behaving as I would hope. You must continue."

These words bowled me over. I could not believe it: he always bore such severe judgment on me!

I was the happiest of slaves, I did not deceive my Master. The man whom I love was proud of me. I had wanted to reply: "But all this is nothing, adored Master, order and I will obey. I want to surprise you so that you will place me above all other slaves known until now. I am capable of enduring everything in order to simply know that I have earned your confidence and your respect. Be happy, my adored Master, and if your happiness must pass through my downfall, I am ready to accept it when I know that by lowering myself before others, I grow in your esteem and in your heart."

What did it matter that Master Julien used my mouth like that of a whore? Or that he mistreated me and drenched me for his pleasure? I was the proud slave of Master Pierre, my revered.

Impatient to be satisfied in his turn, Pierre took the place of Master Julien. He fucked me in the mouth, my tongue serving him as a jewel case. I accomplished that fellatio with a mystic self-communion. During this time, Master Julien used my vagina without consideration. Excited by the sight of the fellatio that I practiced on Pierre, he decided abruptly to use my loins, which, like the whole of my body, were at his mercy. He penetrated without any preliminaries in order to hurt me, and I found the courage not to moan…intensely. I squeezed his penis with my two hands with the same rhythm as the thrusts which projected me forward, towards the one who was at the origin of everything. I thought the trial finished, but a third sex, harder still than the preceding one, forced open the lips of my vagina. I no longer understood. The sudden silence exasperated me, because I was unable to see anything of what happened behind me. I was taken. They penetrated me. I was blind. I recognized neither Pierre, nor Master Julien…and Mistress Maïté was a woman.

When I reconstruct now that scene in my memory, I mock myself for my incomprehensible naively.

I considered myself still as an artless libertine. I didn't yet know everything of the refinements of sadomasochism, nor of the perversity of the men, and less still of some of the women. I knew simply that I loved a man madly in order to follow him blindly into this genre of enterprise, in order to go to the depths of all experiences.

I understood eventually that the member that penetrated me was a strap-on dildo which Maïté had belted around her waist. That audacity excited me. I felt myself melt, my belly liquefied. With an outrageously vicious vocabulary, she demanded that I arch myself further, that I offer myself so that she could penetrate me to the hilt. I yielded to the impetuosity of an orgasm that I would have wanted to be able to control, simply because it was the first time that a woman had penetrated me in that way, just like in the photos in pornographic magazines that had been given me to flick through, cheeks flushed and my belly taught. I came with the certainty that Maïté herself knew the pleasure in bayoneting me as if she had been a male, one of those males whom she liked to train so that she could humiliate them in their machismo.

Drained, some drops of sweat spattered on my shoulders, Maïté pulled it out of me like an animal after coupling and helped me from my prison. After leading me to the bathroom, where she showered me as if I was a child, she ordered me to go and rejoin the two men.

Thus, I was the object of pleasure of these two men and this woman. Maïté seemed warmed up all of a sudden. She approached me, lay me on a bed, spread her legs above my face and demanded irritably that I lick her like a bitch. I lapped her intimacy with absolute submissiveness. She was sweet, and this fresh contact enraptured me. The muscled thighs of a mature woman spread beneath the pressure of my tongue and teeth. She opened her sex further and released herself violently into my mouth. Surprised by that genuine ejaculation, I felt a new orgasm possess me. I was brutally aware that I was coming without the authorization of my Master.

Eventually, we returned to the main room with the nonchalance and good mood that pleasure gives when pushed to its culminating point.

I pressed myself into Pierre's arms, profiting from a moment of inattention from our hosts, because displays of emotion have no place in this type of evening, and I told him, as if I was drunk, that I should never love anybody else but him.

It was now very late, and we had proposed to go and rest, but Master Julien had decided otherwise. He dragged me roughly into the kitchen, slammed me belly down on the long farm table and ordered me to spread my thighs. With an unexpected thrust of the hips, after having observed the indecent sight that I offered despite myself, he penetrated my rear, crying out in anger: "Take that, little slut. Dirty little female tramp."

I let myself be sodomised by that man to whom Pierre had loaned me, because it was my duty.

After a thorough wash, as if to find my state of free woman once more, as if the make-up of the slave was swept away with the bubbling water which flowed between my thighs, Pierre indicated that it was time to return to the hotel.

Dropping off to sleep in the small tapestry hung room in Jouy, I was the happiest of women. Huddled in Pierre's arms, I slept with a smile. Pierre told me later that this smile of happiness lit up my face and had struck him deep down.

# VI – The Ink of Fantasy

The following day we returned to our friends where fresh trials awaited me. Toward the end of the afternoon, I was prepared in waiting for a couple. I had been warned that Clotilde was a dominatrix, and that she would be accompanied by her regular submissive, Vincent. It was decided that I would not see them and they dragged me into the cellar that I had not yet seen. Pierre had chosen my clothes. I wore net stockings, a small flared skirt which allowed glimpses of my pubic hair and a black transparent blouse that barely masked a black corset of leather set with chains.

The voice of Master Julien suddenly sounded: "May I present to you, Laïka, Pierre's slave. She is here in preparation to become an obedient slave." Pierre blindfolded my eyes so that I was unable to see the invited as they descended into the cellar. Someone asked me to turn around and show my arse, which I did obligingly. They ordered me to approach one of the invited who wanted to touch me and, blindly, I took some steps in the direction indicated. Ice-cold hands touched my flesh, making me shudder. This first contact had surprised me, but I offered myself submissively to the caresses growing more insidious until they quickly became agreeable.

They let me know that several people had come to assist in my training and that each of them was going to give me ten lashes of the whip. I prepared myself for this trial by concentrating on the exertion of will which I would have to show. Training to accept pain is only, after all, a sports training like any other. One can easily succeed in extending the limits and in enduring for a little longer, at each experience, the sensation of suffering which one finally gets used to, especially when, like me, one derives such keen excitement and incomparable pleasure.

I recognized immediately the lashes of the whip applied by Pierre. He has a particular method, both cruel and refined, expressed through a kind of caress of the crop, or the cane, before the sharp smacks, always unforeseeable and discerningly proportioned. My Master knew better than anyone how to train me. After the last stroke, he caressed my inflamed buttocks furtively. That simple mark of tenderness gave me the desire to endure still more in order to satisfy him.

They ordered me to go down on all fours, undoubtedly the most humiliating position for a slave, but also the most exciting for the exhibitionist that Pierre had taught me to be, in all circumstances and all places. I recognized, in their softness, the hands of a woman who began to feel my body. With some adroitness they opened my sex. Soon after my belly was invested with a round and cold object that Clotilde wielded lewdly and at length.

The masters decided then that I must be taken back to the first floor in order to remove the blindfold and enable me to know the others invited to that memorable ceremony. I discovered that Clotilde was a superb young blonde with limpid eyes and a face of an astonishing softness which gave a reassuring impression of joviality. I reflected that she was physically the opposite of my idea of a dominatrix, such as I had imagined.

I was placed again at the hole constructed in the wall, where I had been constrained the preceding day. While they used my offered orifices, Pierre exhibited his reddened sex before my eyes, and I tried to touch it with my lips, then with the tip of my tongue darting around at its maximum stretch. But Pierre, with a refinement of cruelty which managed to excite me, backed away each time I was about to finally reach his cock, obliging me to stretch my neck, my tongue, like a true bitch coveting a bone. I heard some humiliating comments on my stubbornness in wanting to lick the cock of my Master. These insults, added to the blows which shook my sex, and fingers which penetrated my body from every direction, made me reach an orgasm whose suddenness staggered me. I had come as if blown down by a gust of pleasure that nothing could delay.

## The Ties That Bind

Taken by a pressing need, and having asked Mistress Maïté with humility for authorization to take me back to the toilets, I saw myself faced by a brief and severe refusal. Confused, I saw someone carry a small bowl into the middle of the room, and I received from Pierre the order to satisfy my need before the invited assembly.

An irrepressible panic swamped me. As much as I was ready to display my body and to offer it for the pleasure of my Master, or to tame the pain in order to be deserving of him, the thought of surrendering myself to a need as intimate appeared unacceptable to me. I felt genuine humiliation. To show me in that degrading position, even when exhibited or whipped, taken or sodomised, my vanity could be satisfied to rouse desire. But by pissing before the assembled voyeurs, I did not arouse the desire of anybody. On this occasion I became aware of the real pride of the slave, which motivates, and by consequence explains and excuses everything. Indeed, the rites of sadomasochism rest on pride: the pride of the master to possess a beautiful and submissive slave; but also the limitless pride of the slave to awaken the least enviable desires, and thus the most rare to test, by these superior and experienced beings, the masters.

The slight impatience that I read in Pierre's attentive look seemed to act on my bladder, which freed itself instinctively, like frightened young bitches who cannot refrain from urinating on the ground when their master scolds or threatens them. I would never have imagined, some months previously, making a similar choice. I managed to disregard all the eyes of those witnesses fixed on the joint between my thighs. When I had finished urinating, Maïté ordered me to sniff my urine, then to drink it. Unsettled by this new trial, I felt myself on the edge of tears, but not daring to protest, I began to lap up without swallowing the pale and still lukewarm liquid, and to my intense surprise, I felt an undeniable pleasure for this unexpected game.

After having submitted to the looks of the invited, I was brought before Clotilde whose polished boots I had to lick with the tip of my tongue. The seductive young woman rewarded me with a very soft caress, which resembled the gesture one makes when stroking the neck of a submissive animal. To my great relief, dinner was announced.

Vincent remained close to the table. He took on the role of the waiting-maid. I later learnt that he endured these blows stoically, with a violence that I found hard to imagine bearable. He wore simply a little apron and leather pants decorated with studs that opened in such a way that one could see his sex. He was there to serve us. They had installed me beneath a specially adapted seat. It contained a hole in its middle so that the master who sat above could receive the oral homage of the slave placed beneath. Everything here seemed conceived for pleasure. Stretched out on the ground, my head resting on a cushion and supported by a small strip of leather so as not to fatigue me, I applied myself to licking the intimacy of Mistress Maïté. She was not satisfied with only feeding me with her pleasure, but also with oysters that she introduced into her vagina and that I had to suck out. I greedily swallowed the mollusk and its juice trickled down my chin. I then passed my tongue over her lips so as not to lose any drop of that precious shell.

# The Ties That Bind

After dinner we went back down to the cellar. Clotilde demanded I lick her at length before making her come. I darted my tongue over her clitoris and she was not slow in issuing moans and the rattles of a frightened animal. That plunged me into a state of excitement so that I felt ready to do everything they could ask of me, for my own pleasure and for that of my Master, my dear and tender Master. At that moment, I loved him literally to madness. He was the one who permitted me to exceed my own limits, to vanquish my taboos, to know the orgasms prohibited to common mortals.

They sat me on a small stool bristling with a large dildo. In that position my vagina became sore, but it was worse when they asked me to sit on the massive cylinder and make it penetrate deep between my buttocks. I felt my anus torn as I impaled myself on the latex. The tightness of that part of my body made the operation painful. Master Julien set the monstrous dildo in motion and its vibrations penetrated right to the deepest point of my body. The slow rotation of the vibrator gave me an orgasm as intense as it was rapid, and when my Master accelerated the diabolical object, I could not prevent myself from beseeching his pity. They deigned to grant me a respite on condition that I accept that cadence a little later. Then they began to pierce me once more, insisting that I penetrate each of my own orifices. I discovered the extreme pleasure that one experiences from taking oneself. I masturbated. They obliged me to do it. I lost all notion of shame, nothing more held me back. My Master watched me. I saw the intensity of his excitement. I was no longer myself, but

I was conscious of my love for Pierre. I was no longer only a body which came with what was imposed on it. I was a slave entirely and I assumed my condition with pride.

Soon my masters wanted to release me. I heard myself refuse, moaning "more, more…" Pierre was exulted. He congratulated me. They increased the speed of the vibrations once more, interrupting them periodically so that I could endure them. I knew then the maddest orgasm that I could imagine.

Pierre, my love, came to join me. He spoke tenderly to me, caressed me gently. I was transported with joy.

I could assist in the training of Vincent. He had knelt on the ground, his eyes lowered, and was masturbating slowly, obeying orders which intimated him to slow down the rhythm of his ignominious caress. They ordered him to come and, almost immediately, he released a jet of semen which spattered the stone flags. He was obliged to lick it up right to the last drop. Then it was decided by the reunited masters that Vincent must be corrected for having ejaculated so abundantly. He received, without wincing, strokes of the crop which lashed his buttocks with long violet slashes. With each blow, Vincent thanked the one who had struck him, and I saw his erection slowly be born again. I was astonished by this spectacle, the first at which I assisted as a witness. *Voyeuse* would be a more appropriate term, because I discovered the surprising pleasure of watching the humiliation of a slave, which transforms quickly into sensual delight.

Afterwards, we returned to our hotel, where we recuperated our strength for the last session, and planned for the following day.

When we returned to the mansion, Pierre promised me in front of Master Julien and Mistress Maïté that this day would be unforgettable for me. I found myself attached to a Saint Andrew's Cross, formed in part by one of the beams. Pierre began to whip me. He flogged my whole body, dwelling on my buttocks, to which he declared devotion like a true cult. Then it was the turn of Master Julien and Mistress Maïté to do me the honor of beating me. They unfastened me before placing me in the iron collar so that my two orifices were made perfectly available, ready to be invested. The first penetration was made extremely painful by the irritation of my mucosa. They ordered me then to lay on the ground and to lift my legs up so that each could take me easily. I was possessed by all the invited, who followed one another in a chain.

I offered myself. I spread open like a flower. I was no longer my own master. I belonged to my Master.

The fire crackled in the old fireplace, making the atmosphere still more torrid. Some ritual instruments were placed in close proximity to the fire. They were genuine branding irons, of diverse dimensions, like those used for branding animals. Mistress Maïté approached me brandishing an iron which had reddened in the embers.

Real terror overwhelmed me. I was not prepared for this trial, which would be unbearable enough for hardened slaves. I trembled from head to toe, beseeching Pierre with a look, but being too proud to exteriorize my fear. Fear of mutilation, of pain, of knowing my body would be marked for life. Fear of crying out, fear of displeasing, fear of deceiving, fear of my own fear that I disavowed…

Pierre's look did not respond to my supplication. Maïté leaned over the proffered buttocks that Master Julien held still. I could not hold back a cry of terror when I thought I felt the burning on my sensitized flesh. I perceived a slight pressure, a sharp and very dry pang, and that was all. I was well and truly marked, but only with black ink. The rite was to provoke my fear, but not to mark me really. I was at once relieved by the unexpected outcome, and secretly disappointed, perhaps, to not have been able to give a new and definitive proof of love for my Master.

# VII – The Pride of the Slave

Here is the letter of submission I sent to Mistress Maïté and Master Julien after that memorable meeting.

*Dear Mistress, dear Master,*

*I am writing to you to tell you how happy I have been to know you and to number among your submissives.*

*With you, and thanks to you, I would like to become the most deserving submissive that you have ever met, docile, obedient and grateful.*

*I would like to share fresh experiences with you. I would like to relive moments as strong and intense as those that we experienced in*

# The Ties That Bind

the course of the weekend.

My dream is always to try to go further in this field and I would like this apprenticeship and progression to be made near you and with your help. I would like to become someone' to go to the limit of my fantasies, beyond the desires of Pierre, without ever being afraid. To be able to confront everything without any apprehension.

Confidence in partners is essential in this field where skin-deep sensitivity is sometimes severely tested.

I would like you to help me be the best, in honor of my Master Pierre, my Love, and in the name of that Love for which I feel no limit.

I want to learn from you what being a perfect slave signifies, a slave whose Master will stretch her pride. To learn everything still unknown to me.

I would like you to make me submit to the worst tortures and humiliations by letting me be confined for several days as you suggested last time. I would wish to be used and displayed as a submissive and docile bitch, so that my character submits to such demands.

I have a vital need to have trust in myself. I have the impression that through that submission I am proving to myself that I am capable of enduring the worst, and I find then an equilibrium which strengthens me.

I would like to see you again soon.

I send you my most perverse memories.

*Laïka*

# VIII – The Captivating Cellar

That evening we were invited to the house of a long standing friend. I did not yet know him, but I felt that Pierre had a particular feeling for him. I knew nothing more. Pierre wanted to keep an air of mystery around the meeting with a master well known in the SM milieu, and that was enough to excite my curiosity into hoping to learn much from the future relationship.

He was called Didier, and his wife, Fiona. I had had the chance to look at photos of her and I found her very beautiful.

We arrived at Gaillac one Saturday evening. Pierre had described Didier as a very perverse being, knowing how to reconcile graciousness and severity in training. The first impression he inspired in me was strange. He had the face of a jolly child with such a cordial way of welcoming us that it embarrassed me.

We entered the main room and I then discovered a delightful man. I listened to him talking. I was somewhat under his charm and I sensed he was going to please me. But I had not come to be under his charm. I was there so that he submit me and train me. I remained silent, paralyzed by apprehension, despite his graciousness and sweetness.

I retreated into silence, a unique refuge which sheltered me from my awkwardness which was due to my lack of confidence.

Fiona was not yet there. I always wait impatiently for the presence of women to reassure me.

Master Didier drew me to him and led me towards the cellar. Pierre followed us in silence along the narrow passageway which led there, just like in the best horror movies. As a matter of fact, we had to go back out of the house and creep into a small stone passageway, and despite my slim waist, I had to squeeze myself through. I was afraid, and Fiona's absence unnerved me. I felt so tense that, if Pierre had not personally known Master Didier, I would have asked to leave without delay. A large oak door was opened and I was amazed to discover the solemn setting of a mystical place.

I was struck by the beauty of this place. It was a magnificent vaulted cellar with exposed stone walls. Candles adorned each of the corners and the flames of the long white candles trembled on the gold-colored age-old stones, making sinuous and menacing shadows leap about. It was so beautiful!

I was fascinated by the nobleness and the sense of predestiny present in that place. That cellar seemed to have been conceived on the first night of time for pleasure and suffering, for the most secret rites, and I conjured up, shuddering, black masses and other prodigious rituals. The bronze light tainted my skin; my body seemed to be impregnated with golden powder. I felt myself to be irresistibly beautiful, and I believe that that evening, particularly, I was. Master Didier encircled my forehead with a blindfold of black velvet. He bound my ankles with strips of leather, rebound by chains to the stone walls. Then he seized my wrists, which he spread cross like, as also my legs, and imprisoned them in the silver bracelets hung from chains fixed directly to the central beam of the vault.

I was then offered to my masters. I was going to be whipped in that humiliating position—arms and legs spread—but the light managed not to make me look indecent.

I had had time to glimpse the impressive collection of accessories arranged on a small table in monastic style. In one corner there was a confessional bearing a hole in its door, inspired by American 'glory holes' and intended, I now know, to receive the member of the man who desires to be honored by the mouth of the slave hidden behind the confessional panel. Thus he would never see her, just as the cloistered slave only sees the sex of men she is bound to honor.

As I received the first stroke of the whip, I realized that it was a supple strap, used as a means of warming my body in advance of other more aggressive strokes. From the strap, Master Didier passed to the riding crop. I recognized the particular bite in the hollow of my back.

# The Ties That Bind

It was a long and thin crop, with a deceptive flexibility and an almost reassuring look. Handled with precision and nuance, each stroke received seemed to me different from the preceding one, depending on whether the flick of the leather struck me flat, or with the whole length of the stem. Master Didier whipped me with a pitiless rigor and I forgot all my good resolutions, crying out beneath the intolerable bite of the lashes.

I perspired abundantly; my body became taut in a silent, but evidently eloquent, supplication. As I now know, the pain which racked me changed slowly into pleasure, and I told myself that I was coming, that I was suffering but that I was coming...

As if they had guessed the intensity of my pleasure, which I had concealed as best I could beneath the fits and starts, Pierre and Didier suddenly hooked pincers on the tips of my breasts and the small lips of my sex, pincers with weights that dragged the flesh towards the ground. I enjoyed bearing the pincers on my breasts: Pierre says that I am a breast sensualist. Making me endure my breasts being pinched, sometimes in a very painful way, gives me almost as much pleasure as being whipped. On the other hand my labial lips are very sensitive, and the pincers always make me suffer a great deal, and despite my efforts, I find it very hard to overcome this type of pain. When Master Didier applied the pincers one after another, their weights stretched my skin painfully. I thought I would not be able to endure them. But the fierce will of never wanting to deceive Pierre allowed me to withstand such heavy maltreatment. I concentrated all my strength on another subject capable of making me forget my sufferings and, through this, I succeeded in forgetting the pain when, breaking the nervous tension which made me tremble at the bottom of my chains, Didier announced the arrival of Fiona.

Suspended by handcuffs which cut into my wrists, spread-eagled to feel the painful joints of my thighs, I could not make a movement nor turn my head to see the beautiful woman who was entering the cellar. I felt only her presence, then the sugar-sweet smell of her perfume. A soft hand caressed my bottom, tenderized by flagellation. I experienced an assuaging which not only belonged to the caresses, but to the presence of that superb woman that I had no right to look at, even when Pierre removed the band which blinded my eyes, then liberated my breasts and sex from the collar of lead weights. So that I could not be tempted to turn towards the beautiful stranger, Master Didier placed a crop across my mouth that I instinctively clasped tight.

I was dying to see her. It is sometimes a real torture not having the right to look at those who take care of you at the time of a training session. This frustration both wounds as it is the proof of not existing and, at the same time, excites terrifically as curiosity is a dominant trait, if I dare admit it, in slaves.

Finally, she walked around my spread-eagled body and stood right in front of me. She struck me as more beautiful still than I could have imagined. She was tall, slender, with finesse and maddening class, with a sexy *je ne sais quoi* in her look, the shape of her sensual lips, the length of her thighs, the muscles of her sport-like body. Fiona seemed

## The Ties That Bind

sure of herself and exuded a calm determination which impressed me. Master Didier had informed me that she had been submissive, but I detected nothing which could console me with that idea. She had nothing of a slave about her. On the contrary, she had the carriage of a proud face, a little like a contemptuous princess who had come to survey her subjects. I could not imagine her kneeling or crawling, but on the contrary able to dominate men as much as women.

That evening, she was naked, apart from a thin leopard skin thong which emphasized the curves of her magnificent and bronzed hips. Her thick red mane, her thin face, her sparkling green eyes metamorphosed her in my mind to the fantasy of a lioness who was about to devour me.

Master Didier approached, a curious appliance in his hand. It was both an electric drill and a miniaspirator. I learned later that it was a very special vibrator that the master had brought in from the United States. He switched on the electric mechanism which produced a humming sound. Then Master Didier placed the suction cup over my clitoris, exposed by my spread-eagled position. A dizzying shiver went through me instantly, as if I had been plugged into an electric current, very sweet and yet unbearable at the same time. I felt the tips of my breasts become erect, my sex liquefied and my eyes burst open with surprise and horror because I understood that if Master Didier didn't stop the mechanism immediately, I was going to piss myself through pleasure, like a stark beginner. I whimpered like a bitch, which incited the master to increase the pressure of that infernal instrument at the centre of my thighs, thighs which trembled like a nervous wreck. Then, abruptly, he interrupted the tension, turned off the apparatus and I found myself suspended in emptiness, a flagellant still standing, agitated by tremblings, a heart beating fit to burst, a sex soaked to the point that I thought for a moment that the juices ran as far as my thighs. I slowly regained my breath, during which Didier, accompanied by Pierre, walked behind me to inspect my body and the havoc provoked by that infernal vibrator. I felt fingers gloved in latex spread my lips, introduce themselves into my intimacy, evaluate the involuntary wetness that contact with the apparatus had generated. Then my cheeks were spread and I was aware of the flash of an electric bulb as I was inspected still more intimately with the latex fingers, and finally with a speculum whose cold steel drove my anus crazy as it opened slowly at the mercy of the instrument which expanded it painfully. I heard the humiliating commentary of Pierre and the opinions of Master Didier on that secret part of mine, which had never been violated in this way before.

Didier restarted the vibrating mechanism, leaving the speculum open between my thighs. The dizzying tension returned in me instantly. Then he said to me: "Profit from it, you have the right to come!"

I obeyed; I came like a demented one. I came freely, without holding back, without being able to stop myself. I was no longer myself. I had never felt my sex react thus. It flowed with a pleasure that I could do nothing about. The lukewarm liquid trickled down my thighs and that new sensation was both humiliating and pleasing. Pierre and Didier were about to bear proof that I was only an object deprived of will, incapable of containing myself, incapable of refusing orgasm. My Master brusquely interrupted my pleasure with these words, "You are indecent, Laïka!" but that only increased my coming…

They unfastened me to let me take a short break, but that interlude lasted only the time it took to prepare the rack on which they ordered me to place myself, which I did obediently and with grace, for the moment had come when Fiona was going to occupy herself with me. She began by caressing me at length with the thin whip of plaited leather that she had at her wrist, held there by a thin tag. She amused herself with my sex, rousing my clitoris, spreading my flesh, penetrating me with the handle of her crop. Then she caressed my open body with an astonishing softness, releasing fulgurating fantasies where thousands of women, who all looked like her, collapsed on me violently and with frightening cruelty.

I dreaded a little the moment when Fiona would decide to use the latex accessories which were lined up in the most menacing fashion on a low table covered with a black shroud. I had seen them out of the corner of my eye during the brief halt which had permitted me to regain my calm. They were all manner of sizes, all manner of textures, and each had a strange form appropriate to the orifices and sensations that it had to invest or release. The most terrifying measured more than forty centimeters long and the fingers of my hand could not go round it. To be truthful, I found these virility substitutes distressing.

In my mind, they represented a degree of obscenity and perversion that an authentic sadomasochist accessory did not have.

As I dreaded, Fiona grasped an instrument of inflatable latex whose function she tested in front of my scared eyes. Worked by a bulb, the body of the penis inflated steadily until it attained a spectacular conical size, which made me fear for an accidental splitting.

With sweetness and determination, Fiona inserted the apparatus in me and began, staring at me intensely, to proceed with the inflation which expanded inexorably. The sensation, although painless, became well and truly unbearable. I had the impression that my sex was overstretched and that my intimate flesh would become distended and would spill out under the invasion of the enormous conical cylinder which seemed to be driven ever deeper into me. I experienced a real disgust in not being able to control the throbbing orgasm which climbed within me, proving to me, if need be, that I really had become what Pierre wanted me to be: a total nymphomaniac, a servile animal at the mercy of the most sickening enjoyments. Despite the pleasure which inflamed my intimacy, I felt myself humiliated by my sexual dependency on that rubber cylinder which was meant to bring me as much emotion as the sex of my Master. In my mind I refused all other orgasms than the one that Pierre gave me when we made love, but I was sensitive to the traces of experience so that my will was gradually giving in, and I was becoming more and more receptive to the practices which, some months earlier, would have literally made me sick.

A theory was born in me that overturned my whole education.

## The Ties That Bind

Essentially, would it not be better to gain pleasure without attaching any importance to the way in which one can or must gain it?

Pierre interrupted my meditations by ordering me to kneel and receive lashes of the whip with which he marked my breasts—long slashes that I could be proud of displaying for a long time.

I bore the scars of the reality of my love. I like to contemplate in a mirror the traces left on me by the lasting proofs of these sessions of submission to the loved one. I detail the abrasions, the streaks which zebra my pearly skin, and I review the intense moments of abnegation as if these regenerated me and made me be reborn more beautiful and better loved.

Today, I am another person. I have changed considerably. I have learnt to control myself, to repress my aggressiveness and, in particular, to communicate. In fact, these practices constitute a new language of the body. It is a new means of expression that Pierre has revealed through our fabulous sadomasochist experiences.

After that Fiona penetrated my behind with a new object, thicker, but very short, which she decided to leave in place until the end of the evening. We went to eat in the immense dining-room, where a fine meal was served. We were all famished. By surrendering to the sin of voracious hunger, by delighting in the *pate de foie gras* and mushrooms, I forgot my condition. However, I sat at the table, my breasts bare, impaled on the latex object, which had the effect of expanding my usually taut orifice, in order to facilitate the penetrations which I would submit to readily later that night.

## Vanessa Duriès

I retain a special memory of that visit to the magic cellar, as if something occurred, between Fiona, Didier and us, which went beyond simple ritual and took on an importance that the future would confirm.

# IX – Failures

Living life to the full sexually, if one departs from the furrowed and beaten track of others, is a luxury not accorded to everyone. Sexual freedom is more of a media concept than a reality in the depths of France. And it is still more delicate in the territory where we unravel, Pierre and I, the fantasy of fantasies, the apotheosis of sexual freedom for many people conditioned by a restrictive upbringing—I know what I speak about. It is a world which arouses both desire and dread, indeed disgust, with the uninitiated who often hang around sadomasochism as if she was a beautiful prostitute, without finding the courage to grapple with her. The principal confusion of these strangers, in what concerns the delights of black leather, lies in the confusion that they make between ritual and the emotional and

## The Ties That Bind

psychological positions of the master and his slave, and the banal exchange practiced by hasty couples who have only gathered together to test their jealousy, their loyalty or their corruptibility. We have never given in to the pressures of exchanges which sometimes hide behind the so-called 'invitation, SM-style.' This has been the cause of some disappointments and bitter deceptions.

How many times have we been deceived by those opportunists who tried to find in submissives a willing recipient of their own debaucheries? The cliché of the female slave loaned by her master makes a good number of loners with evil perversions salivate, who fantasize about being alone with the slave in order to dispense their overflowing frustrations, which they accompany with a plethora of contempt and insults. Pierre does not hesitate to cross France in response to an invitation that he considers interesting. Sometimes we travel 2,000 kilometers in the course of a weekend in order to celebrate with some friends a 'feast of leather.' Yet how many kilometers do we travel to find ourselves again faced by cunning and sly individuals whose only desire is to use the beautiful slut that I become for others, in the very precise context of the world to which Pierre has initiated me?

False mansions are in reality a series of rather banal bedrooms, false ritual evenings initiated by old bachelors deprived of 'cooperative' women, false masters without authority; false perverts without fantasies. Lying publicity is all too common in the surrounds of pure and hard sadomasochism.

It is necessary to include the thick brutes who try to dominate by thumping; the mentally ill who tie up their prey and abandon them for hours in order to masturbate secretly due to their inability to participate in anything; the crooks who ask for money to use 'their equipment' which is really a vague collection of knocked-together kitchen utensils; the frauds who loan the services of a professional to make believe they form a couple of initiates; the inevitable deceivers who arrange meetings at the other end of the country and then never turn up. All these, through their inherent cynicism towards their own primary libido, and their own sexual culture which they have reduced to nothing by reading a few pornographic books from the supermarket, in fact only want a quick fuck.

This widespread sexual misery comforts us in our choice: sado-masochism is an art, a philosophy, a cultural space prohibited to liars and sworn hypocrites.

# X – Slaughtering

During one weekend spent between Paris and Versailles, I had the curious sensation that time had stopped in order to prolong the present.

We had been invited to Versailles by a dominant couple in their forties. We had already met Patrick and Ghislaine in Sarlat, then at the *Cap d'Agde*, and we had seen them several times since.

We met near the Palace, on the upper floor of a town building where a small discreet room had been specially arranged for sadomasochist rites. We had never seen anything like it. Pierre and I were dumbfounded by the number and variety of instruments assigned to the celebration of rites and trials. I was fascinated by this modest den of about thirty-five meters square, which alone contained more objects than all

## The Ties That Bind

the dominants we had ever met possessed. There was an impressive collection of straps (with handles of leather, cord, metal and ivory; with lashes plaited, leaded, garnished with points, in cord and even in velvet), of whips (from all periods, some had been bought in antique shops or gained from private collections or slave prisons from foreign countries), racks (bought from the authentic torture chambers of a chateau in the Massif Central) as well as an exhaustive collection of vibrators, godemiches and other dildos (one dating from Ancient Egypt).

Our hosts informed us that the evening would be spent in Paris at the home of a famous dominatrix, highly respected for the refinement of the treatments that she reserved for slaves who had come from all around the world to meet her.

Alexia! I had heard the most flattering and interesting comments on this emblematic figure of sadomasochism. I was sure that it was her, and the prospect of meeting such a leading light in this world awakened my anxiety and natural shyness.

As soon as we arrived, they took care of blindfolding me in order to increase my anxiety. My excitement was such that I secretly thanked my Master. Rare are the slaves who receive such marks of honor.

I found myself sitting in a comfortable leather armchair, probably in the main room. My thighs were spread by a soft hand and a docile tongue paid homage to my intimacy. The diffused pleasure given by that greedy mouth did not last long. I was soon grabbed and dragged, then pushed against a wall where I was severely whipped without any preparations. Before I could even savor the pain, I was lifted onto a table on which I was stretched out and securely attached. My nipples were squeezed by pincers connected to pulleys which stretched them painfully at the slightest movement.

I abandoned myself gently to this new 'torture', and I relished the strange happiness of submission. I became again what I wanted to be, a simple object at the service of the Master I loved, the object that every man could lust after, surrendered to the pleasure of my Master who could dispose of me and give my body to whoever he wanted. So I was myself, but, at the same time, I was not entirely myself, because I did not belong to myself any longer.

I had climbed a new step in the slave hierarchy. That evening I had received my letters of distinction by being trained by a great dignitary of the dominatrix order. In the mental structure of a slave, that is worth all the torments, all the flagellations, all the offences.

Pierre took me savagely in front of the witnesses of my decline. I offered him my intimacy. He took me violently, brutally, regardless of me, but I liked that. I could no longer do without these plunderings, brutal and violent, but impassioned.

Returning from Versailles, Pierre decided to try a certain number of objects placed at our disposal in the room where we had to sleep. He used me and my body in all positions. I found it exciting to be taken no matter how, no matter by what, provided that the object of offence had a cylindrical form. Late into the night he still made me come several times with the aid of an electric vibrator and with suction cups that left me for dead.

## The Ties That Bind

The following day, I had to be put to a slaughtering. I was still ignorant of what that expression exactly meant. As always before an unknown trial, I was afraid of not being worthy of my Master and of disappointing him. The day passed for me with indescribable anguish, and when evening arrived, I was anxious and excited, hoping that the trial would be as high as my ambitions to push forward the limits of what was unbearable to me. I was blindfolded, then attached to a table, arms and legs spread wide. Master Patrick explained calmly to the unseen hosts that I had traveled more than 600 kilometers to be taken like a whore. The men came close and I suddenly felt a dozen fingers touching me, entering me, exploring me, expanding me. That seemed absolutely intoxicating to me. I experienced a heady pleasure in being exhibited like this before these strangers.

My anxiety vanished completely. For the love of my Master, I could become a perfect whore, the absolute whore, without will, without conditions, without feelings.

Master Patrick bluntly interrupted the session which appeared too soft to him, generating pleasure for me which I did not yet have the right to. I was unfastened to be placed on the rack. There I waited a few minutes in the ignominious position of the whore offered and consenting before unknown sexes began to penetrate me. I was then excavated, ransacked, maltreated and sodomised. I had become a thing mute and open, a real slaughterhouse whore, according to the will and pleasure of Pierre.

Is it the worst insult for a young girl raised in the hypocrisy of the conventional bourgeoisie to be called a whore? To become a whore, is it not the cursed fate, the dishonorable disease, a sort of venereal sickness visible to the naked eye, the divine punishment which swoops down on those who put make-up on too young or dress in short skirts? Playing the whore, is it not the supreme taboo of the stuffy bourgeoisie, who gather together in their highly polished drawing-rooms on the occasion of a bridge party for distinguished citizens? Well, at that precise moment, I had become a whore, I was being the whore.

The shock of this revelation upset me to such a degree that I could not withhold my tears. Was I lost? How could I feel this insane satisfaction in lending my body as if it was an object of no value?

Having guessed the conflicting impulses which were shaking me, Pierre interrupted the session immediately, took me from the room and quieted me down with some soothing caresses and reassuring words. He reminded me that our complicity was exceptional and gave to our love a value, a richness that the others could not suspect. I swallowed my sobs. I had no right to doubt him because everything that Pierre prescribed was wanted also by me. Everything that he imagined corresponded to my fantasies and, undoubtedly, unconscious ones, because I know that since my childhood I have been an eternal rebel and nobody has ever succeeded in imposing on me anything I did not want or desire. Sometimes I have not had the courage to admit this to myself.

When I had regained my self-control, I asked Pierre to lead me back into the room where the men were waiting for my return. I

## The Ties That Bind

appeared blindfolded again, naked, straight and proud, guided by Pierre, who directed me to the circle of excited men. It was me who knelt to take their cocks in my mouth, one after another, until they had all come and poured themselves on my face, my hands and my proffered breasts.

The evening ended in a famous exchange club in the Parisian suburbs. I was dressed for the event with net stockings, a harness, a leather brassiere and a hood made by the hands of Master Patrick himself, who had offered it to me just before entering the club, reputed for the quality of its leather nights. The hood imprisoned my neck, blinded my eyes, only letting air enter by an opening made near my mouth, which, in that way, could always be available if someone wanted to use it. I perceived presences, guessed the heaviness of the looks which seemed to stick to my skin, particularly between my thighs where the magnetism of all those eyes directed at that precise point provoked a burning sensation. The black velvet hood protected my anonymity. I could do everything because of it. This feeling reduced my shame and I asked my Master for authorization to urinate before the guests sitting at tables in the small restaurant which adjoined the bar and meeting room. Proudly, Pierre held the champagne ice bucket on which I crouched and pissed, much to the alarm of the waiter who had witnessed all excesses previously conceivable in this privileged place.

Pierre kept a hold on my lead and took me to the bar. I moved submissively, still blindfolded, on all fours. He made me climb onto a kind of billiards table where I received a violent spanking which tinged my loins crimson. A male slave was required to lick and soothe my bottom. The tongue of the stranger excited me to the highest degree, and then, when Pierre removed my hood, I saw all these people gathered around me, bright-eyed, lips quivering, hands clutching their cocks or women's sexes, and I gave free rein to my coming, which burst without me being able to control its intensity.

Then I was exhibited in a glass cabin which resembled a peep-show stage. Pierre ordered me to display myself without any sense of decency, accentuating with his hands by opening the most intimate parts of my body. He forced me to raise my head, and I saw through the glass panels a multitude of men, pressed close together, who furiously agitated their sexes until a splattering in bursts punctuated the sequence of my poses as they became more provocative.

I was aware of being the fantasy of all my voyeurs. Me, who had doubted my seductive power so much, I had lit the desire of those men, as well as the women. I had consciously accomplished the task that my Master had designated to me. I had become the deserving slut that he wanted me to be.

# XI – The Chastity Belt

I received through the mail a present that Master Patrick had created for me. It was a chastity belt which I cannot begin to describe. Without fear of banality, I could say that it was simply beautiful, but it was also elegant, threatening, impressive, distinguished…

I wanted to try it immediately, and I pulled it on like knickers. Sitting in front of me, Pierre appreciated the wiggle of my hips, which I exaggerated in order to please him, hoping that this fitting session would evolve rapidly. The chastity belt was exactly my size and its creator, in proper, understandable and effective concern, had made two orifices which would allow cylindrical objects of small dimensions to penetrate.

On Pierre's order I saw to the ritual of housework fitted like that,

# The Ties That Bind

under his attentive and burning look. My Master observed with a sudden passion the way I vacuumed the carpet, leaning forward to help the passage of the tube beneath the rustic furniture which decorates our house.

The time came when I had to leave for my lectures. The intense activities organized by my love and Master did not prevent me from following my second year at the University. I felt sorry to have to remove this symbolic and exciting accessory for fear that one of my friends might discover my harness and therefore the nature of the passion that joins me to Pierre. On the point of leaving, my Master ordered me to remove my knickers so I could go bare-arsed through the streets of the town, as would suit a submissive slave m my condition.

In the evening I waited for Pierre impatiently, trying to guess the program he had imagined to celebrate the beautiful fantasmic object. Pierre asked me about my day and, in a good mood, proposed to take me for the evening to an exchange club in Toulouse. I was delighted at that proposition. I was burning to exhibit myself before the customers, proud to belong only to the one I followed faithfully.

It was the first time that Pierre had invited me to the Baskin. The decor was completely unusual. A chrome metal cage embellished with chains occupied the centre of the dance floor. I was impatient to show strangers the beauty of my harness.

Pierre told me I was particularly gorgeous that evening, and I was moved by the compliment, which also gave me a little more confidence. I was wearing black stockings with seams, the chastity belt and a jacket of black silk whose vastness allowed my intimacy to be viewed. A dog collar, embossed with silver, and set with a small ring intended for the snap of the lead, gave my costume the most beautiful touch.

On the dance floor, Pierre made me adopt provocative poses and, feeling intoxicated by the new proof of complicity that he was expecting from me, he ordered me to arouse the desires of strangers and to play with fire. I was doing so well that I became quite obscene and vulgar.

By an artful pirouette I wrapped myself around his arm and removed my jacket. I was naked in front of the dancers, who were struck by amazement. Pierre drew me towards him by my hair. He was passionate. He kissed me voluptuously, making me feel the violence of his desire. Once more he was making me happy by honoring me and surprising me. I was proud; I was feeling chosen and celebrated.

He unveiled my intimate parts, asking in a loud enough voice, so that the speechless voyeurs could hear:

"Who is your Master, Laïka?"

Closing my eyes with composure, I replied:

"You are my one and only Master!"

When the less shy began to come closer to us with the understandable intention of enjoying the spectacle I was offering directly, Pierre made me go down on all fours and withdrew from my chastity belt the long ebony dildo he had placed there at the beginning of the evening. Traces of my excitement were clearly visible on it, and

## The Ties That Bind

my Master ordered me to remove it with my tongue.

Then, having judged that none of the witnesses gathered there was worthy of sharing our complicity—we felt negative and even aggressive waves—Pierre threw my black jacket over my shoulders and we left that place and those mediocre people to be together again amorously.

Pierre often commanded me to wear the chastity belt, depending on his mood and his fantasies.

One day he had the idea to ask me to wear it when I went to my courses. I was astounded. For the first time, I was opposed to him. He asked me where were my beautiful promises of submission. I was his submissive, I must obey him. I held firm. I was an object only for our intense games, but never in daily life. He replied that my whole education would have to be made over again. I did not give in. For the first time, I saw him become angry. We parted without a word. He left. I cried.

I started then to think about it. Was I perhaps wrong to refuse to execute such an easy order? Was I perhaps too sensitive to the symbolism of that object, whose meaning was still barbaric? Was my pride perhaps really stronger than my love? Would it be for him the proof of sublime love? I nourished bitter regrets and dark remorse and was consumed with repentance until the evening. Pierre returned and I threw myself at his feet, promising to accept to wear the belt on one sole condition. He surveyed me from head to toe, and finally asked me what was the unspeakable condition. I begged him to spare me the placement of the 'dildo' (I intentionally used the word that he uses with pleasure to designate the object, as it is one which I do not usually employ). Pierre welcomed my step with a long silence, then signaled grudgingly that he agreed and consented to this proof of weakness.

At university that day I endured the only torture which Pierre could not be part of. I was afraid that someone would guess my belt beneath the tightness of my dress and I removed my coat with extreme shyness. Once seated and attentive to the lecture on American literature, which was about a work by Hemingway, *Fiesta*, I felt the belt becoming very uncomfortable and particularly painful. The leather strip passing between my thighs squeezed my clitoris abominably. I grimaced, which made my classmates smile, but soon I could no longer bear it and I was wriggling like a hysteric hoping to move that awful strip. My friends looked at me several times in surprise. Usually I am quiet and reserved. My agitation eventually alerted the lecturer, who asked:

"Miss Duriès, is something wrong?"

I reddened and assured him that everything was alright. I could not confess that the most sensitive part of my anatomy was tormented by a chastity belt whose model has been directly inspired by engravings dating from the time of the Spanish Inquisition.

# XII – Prostitution

Pierre had assured me that we were going to spend an exceptional and thrilling weekend. I detected in the perpetual need of the masters to be responsible for their programme, the constant anxiety of one day deceiving the one they had subjugated.

Master Patrick and Mistress Ghislaine had invited us for an evening and welcomed us with evident pleasure. I was very happy to see them again, but I took care not to show that feeling as Pierre had taught me. It is always fitting to keep a certain distance in a sadomasochist relationship. Undoubtedly in order to preserve an aspect of mystery, one has to avoid becoming too emotionally involved with one's masters or one's slaves. This is a golden rule applied by the most experienced and which allows relationships to continue in complete independence.

## The Ties That Bind

I found a way to express my gratitude to the couple who received us. In the street that led to the restaurant where we were to dine, I took the initiative to ask Mistress Ghislaine to authorize me to relieve myself in the gutter. This she did, pleasantly surprised. I crouched then between two cars and, as the little bitch I wanted to be that evening, I abandoned myself to the needs of nature, a satisfaction that doubled as I was being observed in this intimate position.

As we were about to enter the restaurant, without having time to ask a single question, Master Patrick pushed me into the entrance hall of the adjacent building and handed me a Walkman, ordering me to listen to the tape inside and follow the instructions to the letter. Slightly panicking at the idea of facing this unexpected trial, I tried to intercept Pierre's look.

Was I going to be alone? Alone facing myself? No, he could not; he had no right to do that to me. I did not deserve to remain alone? What would I do?

Pierre, stay with me, don't leave me! Without you, I'm nothing and you know it. Don't leave me alone. I couldn't do anything. Without you, I won't succeed. Without you, nothing is possible.

My legs began to tremble. Around me, everything was falling apart. I no longer knew anything. Would I have the strength, the courage, to press that 'on' button and listen to the instructions?

I stood there bewildered. Everything was turning upside down in my head. Finally, I thought of my Master, my love, and, above all, of the pride he would feel, and that I should feel, when everything would be done, and when I would be able to tell him my story.

Once I had managed to control the pounding of my heart, I pressed the small button marked 'on' and listened to the tape. The words and sentences of Master Patrick started. Here, word for word, are the orders I received:

"In the entrance hall, press the button marked with the name Albert. Take the lift to the second floor. It is the door on the right. A very pretty young woman will open it, and you will undress her and make love to her without getting undressed yourself. Then you will receive a man with whom you will have to behave with kindness, tact and elegance. You will make him enter the room and ask him for the sum of three-hundred francs. Ku will unfasten his trousers before taking his clothes off. And you will order Valérie to undress you. She will masturbate him at your request and, when his penis is sufficiently erect, you will take it in your mouth. Then you will stretch out on the bed, taking care to spread wide your legs. Lying on the bed, you will offer yourself to him in order to e taken like a whore. Don't forget you are a whore. Once he has taken you, Valérie will lick you until you come in her mouth. Then you will go together into the shower where the man will urinate on you. That is his fantasy. You will accept it without a word. Then you will urinate on Valérie and she will (do the same on you. Accept that and accomplish your task like a whore worthy of the name."

I pressed the button on the intercom, without which nothing could start. My hands were shaking, and I felt my whole body more vulnerable still.

## The Ties That Bind

No voice responded, but the door opened. I walked through the entrance to the building and moved towards the lift. There was still time to turn back, but now I did not want to. I knocked on the door without even being aware of it. I was suffocating, but a gorgeous young woman appeared. She was really superb and was probably my own age. I was at the height of emotion, of excitement too, because the program of everything I had to accomplish with Valérie suddenly appeared very pleasant, but I made my first mistake. I forgot to undress her. She did it herself, with grace and naturalness. Her body was absolutely perfect and I suddenly felt inhibited. I know my own imperfections, which Pierre does not fail to criticize cruelly when he is angry. I would have willingly abandoned myself to her caresses if I had not received the order to lick her. It was difficult to escape her embrace. I felt clumsy, irresolute, tactless; unable to take the initiative as I was supposed to do. I had to react, if I did not want to commit a second error. I began to kiss her soft and moist sex, delicately perfumed, when there was a knock at the door. Valérie seemed surprised by the visitor. My client was introduced.

Catching my reflection in the mirror, I understood why Pierre had insisted categorically that I dress in the costume I was wearing. My stiletto heels gave me the look of an elegant whore ready to receive her client.

The man was there. He had come to pay for the pleasure we would give him.

I heard myself asking for three hundred francs. The man, whose name was Alain, is a regular with prostitutes. It was in my interest not to fail. With a saucy smile I began to unbuckle the belt of his trousers, following the instructions on the tape. Valérie finished undressing our client and took his sex in her slender fingers. She was masturbating him slowly, rolling her palm around the fleshy cylinder as if she was kneading the mixture for a cake. The movement was beautiful to look at. It was exciting to attend to the erection of that sex. It grew larger and expanded. I was fascinated by the languorous game of Valérie's hands. Suddenly the desire to touch that penis took hold of me. I wanted also to take it between my fingers, feel the hard and burning contact, exacerbate the excitement, because by appropriating the sex, I was appropriating the man. I was there for Alain to satisfy his lowest instincts, his vilest fantasies and I had decided not to deceive him, but to surprise him by my cooperation and the appetite for pleasure which suddenly set my loins ablaze.

The penis was now massive and red, a perfect obscenity. I wanted to wash it but Alain did not leave me the time. After sharply ordering Valérie to stop masturbating him, he ordered me with a nod to stretch out on the bed, and after spreading and raising my legs high, without my being prepared he penetrated me without the least regard. Indeed, since I had seen him, I was waiting for the moment when I would be taken carelessly by this stranger who had gained access to my body only through the power of money. Then he ordered Valérie to adopt the same position, and took her in her turn as brutally as me. I executed his desires, spreading my thighs before going down on all

## The Ties That Bind

fours and hoisting up my rump like a filly on the verge of being covered. I was very excited without thinking of being able to come. I was taken by the role that was required of me. I really felt myself in the skin of a whore. My personality was split in two; I was no longer Laïka, I was the little whore of my Master. Not to come did not bother me. A prostitute must not come. If the character I was playing allowed me to surpass myself, the man and his sex would not give me any real physical pleasure. I was only a nurse, a medical helper, a masseur, a manual worker, venal and paid. For the first time I was going the whole way in Pierre's obsessive fantasy which, until now, I had always refused.

Alain asked in a harsh voice, "Which one of you wants to receive me?" I replied spontaneously that I wanted to. He ordered me then to take him in my mouth while Valérie caressed the part of his sex she could reach. I sucked fervently the blazing cock which bucked beneath my tongue. The object became so large that I had a few difficulties leading it to ejaculation. The penis contracted violently but failed to leave my lips, which were sucking on it with such force that they were able to hold it. He suddenly ejaculated, flooding my throat with a liquid I set my heart on drinking mystically right down to the last drop.

He sent us to wash ourselves and I asked him to accompany us in order that he could assist in our intimate toilet. The bathroom was vast and light. Valérie and I felt at ease accomplishing the last part of our pledge. Alain joined us and before we had time to get under the shower, he urinated on us, splashing us with a heavy and tepid jet. We turned in on ourselves so that each patch of skin received his shower. The excitement which resulted gave me the desire to offer our client the spectacle of a love scene between Valérie and me. I started to rub against her delicate and soft form. I desired her and she desired me. We made love almost tenderly.

The bell rang. Valérie rushed to open the door. I saw her throwing herself around Ghislaine's neck and was shocked at the harshness with which she was pushed aside by her. Valérie was forced to go down on all fours and receive a severe correction. She could not hold back her tears beneath the pain, and the spectacle of that attractive girl in tears moved me strangely.

After a meticulous wash and a renewal of makeup, Mistress Ghislaine ordered us to get dressed again before coming down to dine.

There I rejoined my Master who was sitting with Patrick. I was happy and proud to have accomplished my mission. I proposed to devote the three-hundred francs from my work to a fine champagne.

We went to to finish the evening. Our entrance at the brasserie created a sensation. Ghislaine and Patrick preceded us. Pierre kept me on the leash in the most natural way. I watched the looks of complete astonishment of the customers. With Pierre I was discovering the delightful pleasure of shocking decent people. After all, what law forbids keeping a young girl on a leash, and all its implications, in a public place? Nobody has anything to say about that. And I guessed, beyond all amazement, the lust of some, the jealousy of others, the longing, even desire of certain ones.

## The Ties That Bind

The waiter brought us a bottle of *Dom Ruinart*, my favorite champagne. I produced from my body a shining banknote, and held it out to the waiter, literally fascinated by the plunging neckline which hid nothing of my breasts. Our neighbors were watching us more or less discreetly. Undoubtedly they had never seen a young girl kept on a leash by a man before, attached to the foot of the table and paying for champagne for her friends. We left *La Coupole* in a still more spectacular fashion than the way we had entered. As soon as we stepped over the threshold, Pierre instructed me to go down on all fours to reach the car he had parked right in front of the brasserie.

I obeyed through a taste for the game. I did not fix any limit to my new desire to provoke, to shock. This gave me new confidence in myself. I had acquired the certainty that from now on I could go very far, much further than most of my friends in any other field. I realized that Pierre, my Master, was perhaps only a pretext who catalyzed my emotions, but in this role he was already essential to me.

That evening my only regret was feeling claustrophobic, and not being able to place myself in the trunk of the car as Pierre had asked, in a loud voice, before a stunned couple.

# XIII – Spleen

Love and sexuality are burning lands where sensitivity blooms. I am sensitive, impressionable, I am afraid not to succeed in being myself.

Pierre is a seductive man. He has the look of a dynamic and elegant business man. He is tall and slim, though I think he is not sufficiently sporting. His taste for refined objects turns him naturally towards beautiful things, good cars, fine wines, delicious food...attractive women. That revives my deep-seated jealousy which I only succeed in escaping from during our ritual sessions.

My jealousy does not apply to all types of women. The ones who throw themselves into my Master's arms while playing the experienced nymphomaniac exasperate me the most. I cannot stand women who pretend to know everything about life.

## The Ties That Bind

The condition of slave which binds me intimately to Pierre does not allow me to show my jealousy or my aggressiveness towards any woman that my Master could eventually use, because the women he lusts after are there only to appease his fantasies. He uses them in that way. They cannot possibly imagine they are used as tests to control the nuances of feeling that link Pierre and me.

Pierre is a lover of gorgeous women. I know that, above all, he seeks to satisfy his passion. The pretext of my submission seems to give him all the rights, even the rights of making me suffer in my pride as a woman in love.

I do not accept being confronted by those feelings outside our evenings where the relationship between master and slave annihilates any feelings of possessiveness.

When one woman holds his attention more than another, of course I doubt his love for me. I feel humiliation in my bones when he says that a particular woman is desirable, when he thinks she is beautiful. I suffer when he undresses her and looks up and down her body, when all his being is concentrated only on that body, when he forgets me, when he seems in love, like that, with a passing fancy. I am jealous, my body twists, and I feel the burning spreading inside as venom spreading its deadly poison.

Pierre also has the right to loan me because I am his slave. I accept it because I love him. I draw my pleasure from the one he takes from me, sometimes steals from me. I give him my love. There is perhaps no greater love than abnegation. I am devoted to him.

Sometimes I feel he lends me more easily than he would lend certain objects that he likes. There was a certain book, for example, which I had the tactlessness to give to a friend to read without asking his permission. When I told him, he insulted me with all the contempt one can feel for a slave who deceives or irritates. I was upset and when he saw my tears, as often after unnecessary anger, he softened: he took me in his arms to make me forgive him. The instant after I had forgotten everything.

Human beings complement each other. How could I now cope without such a delicious man? The fiery temperament which fashions certain people attracts because it makes obvious what does not exist in ourselves. I think it is the absolute way to complement each other.

I love this man who makes me suffer without even being aware of it. My masochistic nature is not enough to explain my passionate feelings. He is different. He is that part of me I would have liked to be. I love him for the strength that he breathes into me, to the point of making a young inhibited student into the heroine of bewitching nights that the majority of women will never know.

He hoists me up. He projects me. He increases me while revealing the abyss in my soul, magnifying it. He makes me sublime in my role as slave, making me accept my rank as an object. He has created an indestructible bond between us that nothing will break, especially if we were to part, because if we leave each other one day, if the absence of love moves us apart, if our fantasies died down, then for me, he will become immortal.

# XIV – The Golden Rings

Even if I were to lose my memory, I could never forget my twentieth birthday. That day, an exceptional event, Pierre came to fetch me as I left university. I was joyfully swallowed up by his big and luxurious car beneath the envious looks of my classmates who were gathered on the pavement. He drove without a word, despite my looks, despite my hand that tenderly pressed into his before wandering around the blue wool of his suit. He stopped before the most famous jewelers shop in town and signalled me to get out. Still without saying a word, he took me by the arm and opened the door for me. As if he was expected, an assistant came towards us, carrying a tray of black velvet and addressed us with a slightly forced smile. On the tray there were two golden rings which shone in the diffused light of the shop.

"These golden rings are for you," whispered my Master in my ear. "They are your present for your twentieth birthday. You will be infibulated. I want you to wear these rings on the lips of your sex for as long as I desire."

I welcomed this declaration with emotion. I knew that in sadomasochism customs, the placement of rings was a sort of consecration reserved for beloved slaves and submissives. It was a sort of civil marriage reserved for the elite of a religion who professed love in perhaps an unusual but intense way.

Now I was looking forward to being infibulated, but Pierre decided that the ceremony would happen a month later. This illustrates perfectly the complex personality of my Master. When he grants me happiness, he makes me desire it for a long time.

Finally, the much awaited day arrived.

We met for the occasion at the room of Master Patrick and Mistress Ghislaine, and Pierre made me stretch out on a table covered with a garnet-red damask material. I noticed this detail because, usually, I do not like the color. But in this situation, it gave an obvious solemnity to the sacrifice that would be celebrated on the altar. I could not avoid thinking of the blood which would perhaps trickle in a moment from my sex. The thought of this chilled me with fear and, despite all my efforts to concentrate I could not manage to calm myself. I surrendered to a deep-seated fear, the fear I always have of real violence and the spilling of blood. Ghislaine, who had felt the tension growing inside me, came closer and spoke quietly to me in order to reassure me.

Then everything happened very quickly. My thighs were spread, my wrists and ankles bound to the legs of the table. I resisted, but the left side of my lip was pierced. I experienced a flashing burn. Master Patrick caressed me to divert my attention, and with an imperceptible movement, he placed the little golden ring that Pierre had given him through the pierced lip. He had to part my wounded flesh to enlarge the tiny hole. The ring slid in without difficulty and the burning soon faded. But almost immediately, I felt a fresh burning, far more painful. I began screaming, imploring, mutilated in the most intimate part of me. The needle ripped my flesh. The operation became delicate and more and more painful. The other ring was inserted through my other lip. I felt my flesh pulled, torn, incised, abominable perceptions, blind terror, despair...

I would have liked Pierre to take my hand, look at me, encourage me, but he was too busy shooting the scene and I felt lonely, abandoned and exhibited. Master Patrick told me that the operation was finished and that everything had gone off well.

I felt free, an amusing paradox when one considers that I had just been branded like an animal to signify to everyone that, from now on, I belonged to one man, my dear and venerated Master. And I was prouder than ever to have been chosen by Him.

Pierre took my right hand in his and said I still had another trial

## The Ties That Bind

to overcome. I was very moved. I closed my eyes to appreciate that moment of complicity more intensely, and when I opened them again, I saw that I wore a ring on the big finger of my right hand, attached to my wrist by a very thin chain. My eyes clouded with tears, with emotion, but also with resentment. That chain was for me more difficult to bear than the rings which bruised my intimate flesh. That chain could betray my secret and reveal to everyone the whole nature of my relationship with Pierre. That chain imprisoning my hand was a public confession of my submission to the man of my life. By sharing this secret with everyone around me, I would have felt that I had spoilt its magic. No one would understand. No one could know the authenticity of my happiness. I begged Pierre to allow me to remove it, but it was set and I had to wait for a few days in order that the jeweler, a friend of Pierre's, could place a little device with a screw to allow me to take it off, when my Master gave his permission.

I wore that ring when I went to the university and received many compliments from my friends on this item of jewelry which everybody found very aesthetic. When the questions became too precise on the reason that pushed me to wear such a symbolic object, I invented something. I would say, for example, that its origins were Madagascan and that there, in that country, it acted as an amulet, a protector of love and the passion of lovers.

Since my infibulation, I no longer wear underwear. The flimsiest knickers are unbearable, irritate my flesh and make me endure real torments. Pierre orders me to wear them when I have not been obedient enough and that is really a cruel punishment.

So I go about with my sex naked, even more because Pierre requires me to be entirely shaven, smooth, offered, opened to his desires or those of strangers to whom he assigns me.

# XV – The Black Notebook

I have always had the reputation of being very absentminded. But I did not imagine that my lack of attention would in the end have dramatic consequences on my private life.

One day, I left my handbag in my mother's car. She took it home with her without being concerned about its contents and left it on a table, where my father picked it up and opened it. Well, in my bag was a thick black notebook where I kept my most intimate photos, taken by Pierre and my other masters during sessions, ceremonies and trials. Dozens of colored prints presenting me for the most part naked, but most of the time bound, spread-eagled, or being taken by one or several males. The close shots of fellatio and sodomy alternated with scenes of lesbianism, urolagnia, not to forget the snaps of my infibulation and some 'stolen' photos taken without

## The Ties That Bind

my knowledge by participants in an exchange club on a 'leather' evening.

I noticed the disappearance of my bag only in the morning, just as I was leaving for the university. I felt a real panic invade me. There was nothing else to do but wait for the following day in order to return to my mother's, praying to Heaven that nobody was interested in its contents.

But at eight in the morning, the following day, the phone rang. My mother demanded sharply to see me without delay. I swallowed my fear and proposed to meet her after my classes. She came to fetch me at four-thirty. All day long I had lived in fear at the thought of what would happen.

I made my way towards my mother's car as calmly as I could. She looked at me as if she had never seen me. She had that air I knew only too well, when my father has been harassing and blaming her for the slightest thing and would finally end up insulting her with contemptuous words. Sitting next to her, I felt a kind of nausea. I felt like vomiting in that dread of anger, of her judgment, of her condemnation.

Why do parents always feel authorized to judge their children? Are not the children only what their parents have made them?

Are they not their work?

My mother started the engine and, without looking at me, asked if I had anything to say to her. I replied that there was nothing to say, that everything was very clear. She exclaimed that I did not have to be proud. I provoked her by replying that I could be proud of the way I was living. She informed me that I was spoiling my life. I started to laugh, a little nervously, explaining to her that, far from spoiling my life, I had met a man who understood me, made me happy, and who I loved. She could not refrain from bawling out that I was lying, that he forced me to do all these filthy things, that I had perhaps become a lesbian, that I would end up doing it with animals! She was ashamed for me. I opened the door and fled.

I was angry not to be have been understood, that she had not listened to what I had to tell her. She had deceived me, betrayed me, by adopting my father's case, the case of hypocrisy.

The discovery of these pornographic photos provoked a real family scandal. Each thought they ought to lecture me, to threaten me—even with death!—or to cover me in insults.

I was definitively repudiated. Since that day I haven't heard a word from my family.

The weeks that followed were the hardest of my whole life. I sank into a deep depression from which only Pierre could lever me with the strength of his love.

I love Pierre more than ever. I think that love, whatever its nature, can become a lifebuoy, not a survival beacon!

*I still do not know if Pierre's love is as deep as mine, but I am more aware every day that to love remains the most important thing in the world. I make mine this maxim, taken from a book, Let me love once, rather than be loved all my life.*

## THE END

# Afterward:
# *Photographs of Vanessa*

By
Maxim Jakubowski

By the time I came across Vanessa Duriès' book in a *bouquiniste's* dusty box by the Seine in Paris in the summer of 1994, Vanessa was already dead. I knew nothing of this yet. I read the short novel back in London, intrigued by its intensity and courage, often stunned by the extremes of what we might term perversions its female protagonist endured. It rang true. It felt intuitively like more than just an update of *The Story of O*, another tale of submissive slave and master.

On the back cover of the original French edition, Vanessa Duriès smiles at us, smiles at me, fresh-faced, almost innocent, beautiful, an attractive young girl emerging from adolescence, curly-haired. Could this, I wondered, be the real author of this

## The Ties That Bind

dangerous tale of womanhood defiled and proud? The face, the dark eyes that led me, the accidental reader, into the depths of her soul, as her body stood tall under the bite of the whips, the obscene penetrations of every conceivable aperture, the random punishments, the rituals of torture and humiliation. I strongly suspected something of a hoax. Maybe, Vanessa Duriès and that candid photograph were the cover for a pseudonymous pornographer who had somehow hit a chord somewhere inside me?

There she is, luminous, wondrous and young.

Tell me it isn't so, Vanessa, I wondered.

I rang her French publisher, Franck Spengler, and offered to acquire the rights and get the book translated into English and asked him the obvious questions.

He had harbored the same doubts when the manuscript had originally landed on his desk. But he had met Vanessa Duriès and was soon convinced that not only was she the author of the story, but that it was also one-hundred percent autobiographical.

The book appeared in France in March 1993 and had an immediate impact. Vanessa appeared on various television programs and disarmed interviewers and opponents with her evident sincerity. Here was an attractive young student who had been plunged by the power of love into the most depraved depths of the SM world, and stood proudly by her experiences unashamed, almost defiant; invigorated by her vigorous devotion for Pierre, her master, an older man who had led her into this new, shadowy life.

## Vanessa Duriès

One day, I would like to see video recordings of the programs Vanessa participated in on the occasion of the book's launch. Something inside me beckons the sound of her voice, with a warm Southern regional accent I guess—she came from Agen, not far from Bordeaux; I wish to see the way her eyes must have twinkled under the studio lights, how her body moved in fascinating ways, her lips opened and curled, how the curls of her dark hair fell upon her neck as she defended her experiences head held high. It will be the only chance I will ever have to see Vanessa in motion.

I have press cuttings from her newspaper and magazine interviews from the same period. She is a year older than the back jacket photograph, twenty-one now. The curls in her hair are less evident in this blurry photocopy of a photocopy. She sits on a park bench, her winning smile shyly aimed at the camera, wearing a simple white blouse under her quiet, conservative jacket. She is holding a book, probably her own. She looks like just another pretty French student. In another photograph, even blurrier, she sits again, pensive this time, her gaze directed downwards, her skirt hitched up to mid-thigh; it is possibly the same suit, but here she is not wearing a shirt, the jacket is buttoned and you can see a simple, sober necklace around her fragile neck. She holds her hands together. Under the jacket, I know she is not wearing a brassiere; there, peer closer, are the breasts of Vanessa, the breasts that have been whipped, beaten, the nipples that have been twisted, tortured, pulled to the limits of the skin's endurance, licked, pierced by needles, lovingly caressed.

## The Ties That Bind

Two months after her book's publication in France, in May 1993, Vanessa was asked, I assume by her domineering master, to pose in the nude for a skin magazine, no doubt in another test of her submissiveness. Six more photographs of Vanessa.

The first picture occupies two-thirds of the double-page opening spread, a loving close-up of her face, eyes peering at the lens, a spotlight reflected in her dark pupils, her delicate upturned nose, the sharply drawn eyebrows highlighted by an imperceptible scar where the bridge of her nose begins. Her lustrous hair partly in frame, tousled, brown I know (although all the photographs are in black and white—yet again, cause for infinite regret, that I shall never witness the colors of Vanessa's skin, the shades of her bare flesh). Her right cheek is partly obscured as her face lies on a blanket where the leather strands of a whip are spread-eagled touching her full lips and the underside of her nose. Vanessa watches me, the hint of a naked shoulder trimmed away, a black bra strap breaking into the frame. This is Vanessa, the abominably beautiful Vanessa who allowed utter strangers to sodomize her at will, to introduce foul foreign objects inside her body. This is my favorite shot of Vanessa, the one where she is paradoxically at her most open, naked, receptive. She looks at me from the glossy page, her features almost life size, the pores of her skin crudely magnified.

I turn the pages of the magazine.

On the left page, she appears sitting awkwardly askew on a cloth backdrop holding a riding crop. She is nude, her heavy breasts leaning towards me, the reader, the voyeur, around her neck a collar to which a thin metal chain is attached. The make-up on her face is too harsh (as it is in all the photos to follow), giving her features a hardness which is alien to her nature. She no longer smiles. Her stockings climb up to midway up her thighs. Around both her wrists are thick leather straps connected by a metal chain. For a brunette, her nipples, her areola are surprisingly pale.

The right-hand page is all photograph. A defiant look in her eyes, Vanessa sits legs wide open on a low black table. A dog collar around her neck, her breasts encircled by a complicated leather harness connected in a subtle arrangement of straps to the lower part of her body where her sex is held open to our gaze. Her clitoris is clearly visible, jutting out under the conjugated pressure of the leather bands that surround her slit, inner lips swollen but held together by a metal ring attached to the lower point of entry of her outer cunt lips. She is wearing stockings, a different pair from previously, high heels, still the same straps around her wrists and, in her left hand, holds another whip, seemingly the same as on the opening spread shot. Her pubes are shaven clean, so that the delightful obscenity of her open sex is inescapable, enhanced by the shining ring dangling there. She has thin arms, the veins of her left arm visible as she leans back, thrusting her shoulders forward. Around her waist there is a heavy leather band, adorned with a myriad baroque metal studs.

The waistband is the only adornment left on the next photograph which shows us Vanessa lying downwards on the cloth, her left hand

## The Ties That Bind

holding her breast, her legs upwards, a knee bent, feet cropped out of the shot. Still she doesn't smile Her shaven sex unbearably bare, with a hint of darkness surrounding it, closed. I perversely approach my myopic eyes closer to the photograph and notice a few blemishes, pimples maybe, irritations of the skin from the passage of the razor blade over her shorn pubic area. On the next page, a right-hand side one, another full-page photograph, the most indecent of all, Vanessa on a high-back chair in all her pornographic splendor. Stockings, high heels, and her thighs crucified apart. Another leather harness surrounds her open sex. She holds her arms upwards and pulls a metal chain through her open mouth, between her teeth, the hint of provocation in her eyes. Her full breasts, nipples paler than ever, adorned by a curtain of six metal chains connected to a leather collar that circles her neck and extends into three branches, two on each side of her breasts, holding their weight up by the sides, biting no doubt into her skin, the final branch separating the round globes of her femininity and anchoring the metal chains draped across her offered chest.

She wears the same outfit in the last photograph, a double-page spread which ends the feature, with the final text of the interview that accompanies the photos superimposed in the top right-hand corner. She is leaning on one arm. Her legs are partly open, her sex lips slightly creased by the position, her nipples visibly erect. There is a slight stain on the underside of her left breast; I am unsure whether it is an actual birthmark or a fault in the printing of the photograph. Her full lips are closed, the colors of the dark lipstick surrounding the shape of a perfect kiss. The make-up circling her eyes is too dark, ages her beyond her twenty-one years. There will be no photographs of Vanessa at twenty-two. This immodest pose, as they all were, this brazen exhibition of her body is the last picture we have of Vanessa Duriès, author of *The Ties That Bind*.

Seven months later, on the 13th of December 1993, returning from a festival in Montpellier, in the south of France, which she was covering for a magazine, she died in a car crash, traveling towards Paris, together with three other passengers in the car, two other writers and their child.

She was bringing her French publisher the first thirty pages or so of what she hoped would be her second book, *The Rival*, about the rivalry between two submissive women. Another erotic work which, I am confident, would have assured her of a place in the modern pantheon of erotica. Sadly, we will not read this book.

*The Ties That Bind* is more than a novel, it is a true story. Vanessa's story is touching. It might shock or disgust some; the truth about human nature is never palatable when you have the courage to explore the dark side. Vanessa Duriès had the guts and returned to tell us the story.

Goodbye Vanessa. The images of your sex, your pale nipples and quiet smile, the story of your experiences, will always remain within me, and I will miss you badly.

# AVAILABLE FROM
# MAGIC CARPET BOOKS

## The Story Of M... A Memoir
## by Maria Isabel Pita

The true, vividly detailed and profoundly erotic account of a beautiful, intelligent woman's first year of training as a slave to the man of her dreams. Maria Isabel Pita wrote this account of her ascent into submission for all the women out there who might be confused and frightened by their own contradictory desires, just as she was. Her vividly detailed story makes it clear we should never feel guilty about daring to make our deepest, darkest longings come true, and serves as proof that they do.
0-9726339-5-2 **$14.95**

## Beauty & Submission by Maria Isabel Pita

In a desire to tell the truth and dispel negative stereotypes about the life of a sex slave, Maria Isabel Pita wrote *The Story of M... A Memoir*. Her intensely erotic life with the man of her dreams continues now in Beauty & Submission, a vividly detailed sexual and philosophical account of her second year of training as a slave to her Master and soul mate.
0-9755331-1-8 **$14.95**

## The Collector's Edition of Victorian Erotica
## Dr. Major LaCartilie, Editor

No lone soul can possibly read the thousands of erotic books, pamphlets and broadsides the English reading public were offered in the 19th century. In this comprehensive anthology, 'erotica' stands for bawdy, obscene, salacious, pornographic and ribald works including humor and satire employing sexual elements. Included are selections from such Anonymous classics as *A Weekend Visit, The Modern Eveline, Misfortunes of Mary, My Secret Life, The*

*Man With A Maid*, *The Life of Fanny Hill*, *The Mournings of a Courtesan*, *The Romance of Lust*, *Pauline*, *Forbidden Fruit* and *Venus School-Mistress*.
0-9755331-0-X                                                    $15.95

---

## Guilty Pleasures by Maria Isabel Pita

*Guilty Pleasures* explores the passionate willingness of women throughout the ages to offer themselves up to the forces of love. Historical facts are seamlessly woven into intensely graphic sexual encounters.

Beneath the cover of *Guilty Pleasures* you will find intensely erotic love stories with a profound feel for the different centuries and cultures where they take place. An ancient Egyptian princess… a courtesan rising to fame in Athen's Golden Age…a Transylvanian Count's wicked bride… and many more are all one eternal woman in *Guilty Pleasures*.
0-9755331-5-0                                                    $16.95

---

## The Collector's Edition of The Lost Erotic Novels
## Dr. Major LaCartilie, Editor

The history of erotic literature is long and distinguished. It holds valuable lessons and insights for the general reader, the sociologist, the student of sexual behavior, and the literary specialist interested in knowing how people of different cultures and different times acted and how these actions relate to the present. They are presented to the reader exactly as they first appeared in print by writers who were, in every sense, representative of their time: *The Instruments of the Passion & Misfortunes of Mary*–Anonymous; *White Stains* - Anaïs Nin & Friends; *Innocence* - Harriet Daimler
0-9755331-0-X                                                    $16.95

---

## The Ties That Bind by Vanessa Duriés

The incredible confessions of a thrillingly unconventional woman. From the first page, this chronicle of dominance and submission will keep you gasping with its vivid depictions of sensual abandon. At the hand of Masters

Georges, Patrick, Pierre and others, this submissive seductress experiences pleasures she never knew existed. Re-print of the French bestseller.
0-9766510-1-7 $14.95

## Cat's Collar - Three Erotic Romances by Maria Isabel Pita

*Dreams of Anubis* – A legal secretary from Boston visiting Egypt explores much more than just tombs and temples in the stimulating arms of a powerfully erotic priest of Anubis who enters her dreams, and then her life one night in the dark heart of Cairo's timeless bazaar.

*Rituals of Surrender* – Maia Wilson finds herself the heart of an erotic web spun by three sexy, enigmatic men – modern Druids intent on using her for a dark and ancient rite…

*Cat's Collar* – Interior designer Mira Rosemond finds herself in one attractive successful man's bedroom after the other, but then one beautiful morning a stranger dressed in black leather takes a short cut through her garden and changes the course of her life forever.
0-9766510-0-9 $16.95

# Available January 2006

## Monique, Blanche & Alice

**ALICE:** When innocent young Alice goes to live with her uncle, she has no choice then but to suffer all the deliciously shocking consequences…

**MONIQUE:** A mysterious Villa by the sea is the setting for dark sexual rites that beckon to many a lovely young woman, including the ripe and willing Monique…

**BLANCHE:** When young Blanche loses her husband on her honeymoon, it becomes clear she will need a job. She sets her sights on the stage, and soon encounters a cast of lecherous characters intent on making her path to success as hot and hard as possible.
0-9766510-3-3 $16.95

# The Collector's Edition of the Ironwood Series by Don Winslow

The three Ironwood classics revised exclusively for this Magic Carpet Collector's edition.

## Ironwood

James Carrington's bleak prospects were transformed overnight when he was offered a choice position at Ironwood, a unique finishing school where young women were trained to become premiere Ladies of Pleasure.

## Ironwood Revisited

In ***IRONWOOD REVISITED***, we follow James' rise to power in that garden of erotic delights. We come to understand how Ironwood, with its strict standards and iron discipline has acquired its enviable reputation among the world's most discriminating connoisseurs.

## Images of Ironwood

***IMAGES OF IRONWOOD*** presents selected scenes of unrelenting sensuality, of erotic longing, and of those bizarre proclivities which touch the outer fringe of human sexuality.

0-9766510-2-5 **$17.95**

## Send check or money order to:

Magic Carpet Books
PO Box 473
New Milford, CT 06776

Postage free in the United States add $2.50 for packages outside the United States

magiccarpetbooks@earthlink.net

Visit our website at:
www.magic-carpet-books.com